W9-DFS-016

DEATH
SPLITS A HAIR

DEATH
SPLITS A HAIR

NANCY BELL

THORNDIKE
CHIVERS

This Large Print edition is published by Thorndike Press®, Waterville, Maine USA and by BBC Audiobooks, Ltd, Bath, England.

Published in 2005 in the U.S. by arrangement with St. Martin's Press, LLC.

Published in 2005 in the U.K. by arrangement with Robert Hale Limited.

U.S. Hardcover 0-7862-7641-X (Americana)
U.K. Hardcover 1-4056-3410-3 (Chivers Large Print)
U.K. Softcover 1-4056-3411-1 (Camden Large Print)

L P-M
Bell

A Judge Jackson Crain Mystery

The text of this Large Print edition is unabridged.
Other aspects of the book may vary from the original edition.

Set in 16 pt. Plantin.

Printed in the United States on permanent paper.

British Library Cataloguing-in-Publication Data available

Library of Congress Cataloging-in-Publication Data

Bell, Nancy, 1932–
    Death splits a hair / by Nancy Bell.
       p. cm. — (Thorndike Press large print Americana)
    ISBN 0-7862-7641-X (lg. print : hc : alk. paper)
    1. Judges — Fiction.   2. Barbers — Crimes against —
Fiction.   3. Fathers and daughters — Fiction.   4. Teenage
girls — Fiction.   5. Texas — Fiction.   6. Large type books.
I. Title.   II. Thorndike Press large print Americana series.
PS3552.E5219D43 2005b
    813'.54—dc22   2005007369

DEATH
SPLITS A HAIR

1

Jackson Crain pushed open the door of the Post Oak Barbershop, entered and stomped his boots on the rubber mat to dislodge the snow. A freakish spring storm had blown into town the night before, coating the trees and power lines with ice and leaving a treacherous layer of snow mixed with sleet all over the ground. Joe Junior McBride, his long frame folded over the front chair, was putting the finishing touches on what remained of Horace Kinkaid's hair. He bobbed his head in Jackson's direction and waved his shears toward the row of chairs lined up against the wall.

"Take a seat, Judge. I'll be with you pretty quick here." He picked up a brush and began to brush the clippings off Horace's neck.

Jackson picked up a dog-eared copy of *Newsweek*.

"Ow," Horace complained. "What is that, a wire brush?"

Joe Junior kept brushing. "Don't be such a baby. This won't take long. You don't want hair falling down your shirt, do you?"

Jackson grinned. He had always enjoyed coming into the old barbershop with its tile floor and bay-rum scent. He enjoyed the social aspect of the place as much as anything else. Certainly, he could have gotten a better haircut someplace else, he thought, but it just wouldn't be the same. He had been patronizing the shop since he got his first haircut almost forty years ago. Then Joe Junior's father, Joe Senior, had been the only barber in town. Now all that had changed. A good half the men in town patronized Quik-Kuts out on the bypass or one of the beauty salons that catered to the unisex trade. Joe Junior was doing all right, though. He had a prime location right in the middle of the block in the business district. He would always pick up the bank and courthouse trade — and he was the only barber in town who could style the Baptist preacher's pompadour just the way he liked it.

Joe Junior was a long, tall drink of water. A classmate of Jackson's, he had been a star basketball player and voted most likely to succeed in high school. Everyone thought he'd go to college, using one of the scholarships he'd been offered, but that never happened. On graduation night, he

8

and his girlfriend, Gracie Simmons, had gotten a little carried away — so carried away, in fact, that she found herself pregnant. Against the wishes of both sets of parents, they insisted on getting married and the wedding was held on the Fourth of July. After a short honeymoon, Joe had enrolled in barber college. Joe McBride III, or Three, as he was called, was born in February. If Joe Junior was disappointed by this turn of events, he never showed it. He adored his wife and doted on his son. When Joe's father retired and his parents decided to move to Florida, Joe and Gracie moved into the family home. Then tragedy struck. When the boy was only four, Gracie, pregnant again, was run down and killed by a drunken driver while crossing the street in front of her own house. Two years later, Joe Junior married the lovely Marlene Ashburn, a widow with a young daughter.

"How 'bout this weather?" Horace, editor of the local newspaper, was examining his bullet-shaped head critically in the hand mirror Joe Junior had handed him.

"Weatherman says it's supposed to warm up tomorrow." Joe Junior put his foot on the pump to lower the chair so Horace could stand up.

"Good thing," Horace said, digging for his wallet. "We'll have a power outage for sure if this keeps up." He handed the barber two bills. "Here you go. Next time, I'm having that pretty little assistant you got do my hair. Where is she, anyway?"

"I let Gini stay home because of the weather." Joe Junior put the money in the cash drawer. "She can cut your hair all right, but you'd better not ever let her hear you calling her my assistant. She's a fully certified hair stylist, and a feminist to boot. She'll yank out what little hair you've got left if you patronize her. Step up, Jackson. Shampoo?"

Jackson shook his head. "Washed it this morning. Just give me a trim."

"Fair warning," Horace said. He sat and watched as Joe Junior trimmed Jackson's hair. "Hey, Jackson, what's going on over at the courthouse? This is one hell of a slow news week."

Jackson, who was county judge of Post Oak County, thought a minute. A light note crept into his voice. "There's a leak in the roof. Last time it rained, it got the county clerk's computer all wet. Fortunately, no damage was done. That help any?"

"You know it doesn't, Jackson. I need

real news. Anybody in jail I ought to know about?"

Jackson thought a minute. "Edna's found the Lord. She's decided not to cuss anymore."

Edna Buchannan was Jackson's foul-mouthed secretary.

"Now that would be news" — Horace grinned — "if it were true!"

Joe Junior was finishing up Jackson's haircut. He brushed his shoulders with the soft brush. "I pity you, Horace. Trying to run a paper in this town is a losing proposition. Nothing ever happens worth reporting."

"You sure have got that right," Horace agreed. He suddenly chuckled and pointed to the window. "Would you look at that? Old Rip's done gone ass over teakettle!"

Sure enough, Rip Clark, portly proprietor of the Wagon Wheel Café, had lost his footing and was sitting on the icy sidewalk trying to figure out how to gain enough traction to stand up.

The three men stood at the window watching curiously while Rip tried one maneuver after another to get back on his feet. His mouth was moving and they could only wonder what obscenities were spewing out of it. Finally, Jackson took pity on him. He pushed open the door and approached Rip, treading gingerly on the ice. Wrapping one arm around one of the old-fashioned lampposts the Main Street Committee had erected along the sidewalks, he leaned forward and extended one hand to help Rip. Rip grasped the hand and struggled to gain a foothold on the ice. He almost made it, but his feet slipped out from under him again, and he sat down again, hard, on the ice.

"It ain't gonna work, Jackson," Rip growled. "I reckon I'll be settin' here on this goddam sidewalk until the goddam stuff melts!" He made an obscene gesture in the direction of the two grinning faces in the barbershop window.

Jackson, not being able to think of a response to that, stood holding the lamppost and trying to figure out a solution to the problem. Finally, with a nod of his head, he began to inch himself carefully back to the barbershop. He opened the door and picked up the rubber mat off the floor, then turned and slid it across the ice toward Rip, who caught it and immediately began to manipulate his body until he was seated on the mat. Then, with great care, he got to his feet.

Joe Junior stuck his head out the door. "Come on in here, pal," he called. "I just made some fresh coffee."

Inside the barbershop, Rip took a seat on the shoe-shine bench while the barber went to fetch the coffee. Rip, an old Navy man, was wearing a soiled apron and a white sailor's cap, also soiled, on his head.

"Anybody else?" Joe Junior yelled from the back room.

"I'll take a cup." Jackson pulled a Don Diego cigar out of his pocket and sniffed it appreciatively.

"Me, too," said Horace. "Hey, Rip, don't you ever take that apron off? I'll bet you sleep in the damn thing."

Rip pretended not to hear.

Jackson and Horace seated themselves in the chairs along the wall and waited until Joe Junior came back with fragrant mugs of hot, black coffee. "Hope you guys don't take cream or sugar," he said. "I don't keep the stuff." He took a seat in the front barber chair facing the others.

"Hey, Jackson." He sipped his coffee. "I sure appreciate you letting the young'un practice that horn of hers over at your house. She's a good kid, but she was about to drive us to drink with that thing." Joe Junior's stepdaughter, Ashley, fourteen, played French horn in the middle-school band, as did Jackson's daughter, Patty.

"No problem," Jackson said. "The girls practice up in Patty's room. I can't hear a thing."

The truth was Jackson was more than glad to have Patty at home and under his watchful eye. As she grew older, he was beginning to notice, these times were becoming less and less frequent.

"Mighty good coffee," Horace said. "Rip, you ought to get his recipe."

"Eat shit," Rip said, still smarting from his recent predicament.

Horace got a great deal of pleasure out of aggravating Rip. He took a pad and pencil out of his pocket. "Friend, I'd like to interview you for a human-interest story. What was going through your mind as you lay there helpless as a June bug on that ice?"

"Fuck off," Rip growled.

"Come on, Rip." Joe Junior was in a conciliatory mood. "He didn't mean anything."

"The hell I didn't," Horace said. "My readers like a good laugh same as I do." He drained his mug and set it on the magazine table. "Hey, Joe, anybody ever tell you you look like that actor, Jimmy Stewart? Talk like him, too."

"He's dead," Rip muttered.

Joe Junior ignored this. "A few times.

14

Wife says that's the only reason she married me."

"Too bad you ain't rich like he was," Rip put in.

Jackson changed the subject. "How's Three?"

"Oh, fine." Joe Junior went to the back and returned carrying the coffeepot. "More?" The men offered their cups for a refill. "Matter of fact," he continued, "the kid's starting a new job next week. He's going to work as a fishing guide down on the coast."

"Good. How'd he land that?"

"Not sure." Joe Junior put down his coffee mug. "He's got a friend of a friend that owns a boat. At least I think that's what it is. You know how kids are these days. They don't tell you anything. He seems real excited about it, though. I think he'll do just fine." He picked up his mug again, looked in and saw it was empty and set it back down. "He's doing good — great — in fact."

Jackson wondered just how well the boy was really doing. He had graduated from high school a year ago, and, so far, was still living at home. As far as Jackson knew, he had never been able to keep a job for more than a few weeks at a time, and more than

15

once he'd been in trouble with the law. Jackson felt sorry for Joe. Like most people in town, Jackson liked the barber, with his slow Texas drawl and laid-back manner. He had been pleased when Marlene married him. Jackson had dated Marlene in high school and was still fond of her in a platonic way. She had been, and still was, a beautiful girl and as sweet as she was beautiful. Jackson had to admit, though, that lately she had looked drawn and tired.

Just then, the door was pushed open and a small woman wearing a red parka and fur-lined boots entered the shop. She stomped the snow off her feet and pushed the hood of her coat back to reveal a mop of blond curls and a face that made the men sit up and take notice.

Her skin, rosy from the cold, was the color of rich cream; her lips, painted bright pink, were full cupid bows; and her eyes, Dresden blue, were round, giving her an almost startled expression. They dominated her face.

Joe Junior came forward to help her off with her coat. "I told you to stay home today," he chided. "Did you drive your car here?"

She laughed a throaty laugh. "Don't be an old worrywart," she teased. "The city's already sanded the streets." She gestured toward the three men, who sat staring openly. "Anyway, looks like you can use some help."

"No. As a matter of fact, they're taken care of." He winked. "Maybe you could talk one of them into a manicure, though. Boys, meet Gini McGill."

He grinned at the gaping faces. "Come on, guys, where are your manners? Never seen a pretty girl before?"

"It's not that." Horace got ahold of himself. "It's just that I can't figure out what she's doing working in a place like this."

The others laughed.

"I'm just a small-town girl at heart," she said. "I got tired of fighting the rat race."

"One day, she just walked in here and asked if I needed help," Joe laughed. "Well, look at her. Would you have said no?"

"Well, I got to git." Rip climbed down from the shoe-shine bench. "Muriel's back at the café all by herself."

"Me, too," Jackson said.

"Wait a second and I'll walk down to the courthouse with you." Horace followed Jackson out the door. "That Joe Junior, ain't he a fine feller?"

"Sure," Jackson said.

"Is that all you can say? Just sure? Everybody in town knows he's a fine feller. Look at how he's led the Boy Scout troop for going on twenty years. He's a deacon in his church, and the guy's served on the museum board for God knows how long. What's not to like, buddy?"

"Yeah, okay, he's a good guy."

Horace let it drop.

Jackson was thinking about the time last fall when Marlene had come to him for advice. He had barely recognized her that day. At thirty-eight, she looked fifty. Her once bright auburn hair was stringy and dull, and when she looked at him, her eyes had lost their light. She was tall, almost as tall as Jackson, and had always carried herself like a model. Now her shoulders curved as she sat in the chair in front of Jackson's desk. Tension drew the corners of her mouth down, and lines had formed between her eyebrows. Speaking rapidly and without pause, she had told him that her marriage was over, that she couldn't be married to Joe Junior any longer.

"Why?" Jackson asked, surprised.

"It's Three, Jackson." She folded her hands in her lap to stop them from shaking. "He's ruining our lives."

"Come on, he's just a kid. It can't be that bad."

"No, he's not a kid!" Her eyes flashed at Jackson. "He's nineteen years old."

"Nineteen's still young."

She picked up her purse and rose to go. "I knew you wouldn't believe me."

Jackson came around the desk and gently lowered her back into her seat. He sat on the edge of the desk and looked at her, arms folded. "Don't be silly. Of course I believe you. I'm just trying to understand. Be more specific; give me an example."

"Okay, here's one. Joe told Ashley she couldn't practice her horn at home anymore. And do you know why? Because Three says it interferes with his television!" She took a tissue from her purse and dabbed at her eyes. "Oh, Joe pretended it wasn't that, said she was disturbing the neighbors — but I knew the real reason, and so did Ashley."

"Maybe he was right." Jackson smiled. "Patty plays the French horn, too. Those things can be pretty loud in an enclosed space."

"No, Jackson, it's not that. Ashley's room is too far from the neighbors' houses for them to hear a thing. But it's right next door to Three's room. Oh, it's him all right. I heard him complaining to his dad myself — and I heard Joe say he'd take care of it."

Jackson nodded. "Go on."

"It just breaks my heart, Jackson. You know what Ashley looks like. She's never going to be one of the popular girls . . ."

Jackson did know. Ashley was tall like her mother, but overweight. She wore baggy clothes to try to hide her body, but these only made her look frumpy. He also knew she was funny, easygoing, smart, and his daughter Patty's best friend.

"I wouldn't be so sure," he said.

"Well, anyway, she needs the band. It gives her a reason to feel important. She's good on that horn, and the band kids all like her. If he makes her quit because of that boy's whim, it'll be the last straw. I'll divorce him, Jackson. I really will! He doesn't have any borders where Three's concerned. This morning he told me he's thinking about remodeling the room off the garage so Three can have a place to work on his computer. All the boy ever does is play with the thing. Will you get me a divorce, Jackson?"

"What would you and Ashley do?"

"Oh, well . . . I'd get a job. I'm not afraid to work."

Jackson felt a pang of pity for her.

20

"Marlene, you've never worked. You and Ashley were living on child-support checks and welfare when you married Joe."

"Then you won't help me?" Her eyes flashed.

"I didn't say that. Of course I'll help. Ashley can practice at my house. She's there most of the time anyway." He smiled.

"Thanks, Jackson. That will help a lot. But it doesn't solve the problem. Three's been trying to break up our marriage from the very start — and now I'm afraid he's succeeded."

"Tell me more." Jackson was still unconvinced. "What has he done aside from the horn incident?"

"For one thing, he goads me until I lose my temper. I've always had a temper, Jackson. You know that."

Jackson nodded. Marlene had been fiery all her life, but her flare-ups were gone as quickly as they appeared, and her normally happy disposition would return.

"Well, that boy's learned to push all my buttons, you know? Then I end up screaming at him, and Joe takes his side." She leaned forward. "Every single time he takes his side. Joe used to understand when I said things in anger. He knew I didn't really mean them. Now, he's changed. I'm always the villain." She paused. "And it's all because of that Three! I can't stand it anymore. I'll kill myself, I really will, Jackson." She burst into tears.

Jackson handed her a tissue from the box on his desk, then, reaching behind him, he picked up a memo pad. He jotted down a name and telephone number and waited until Marlene's sobs had subsided. "Here," he said, handing her the slip of paper. "I want you to go and talk to Barry Ernst. He's a good therapist. Hon, you need him more than you need me. After six weeks of sessions, if you still want the divorce, we'll talk again."

She took the paper and slid it into her purse. "I'll go see this man, Jackson, to please you. But no amount of talking is going to change this situation. I'll be back."

This was the last time Jackson had seen Marlene. Three weeks later, Ashley reported that the couple had gone on a skiing vacation in Colorado.

2

Small-town county judges occupy a unique position. Their jurisdictions are limited to issues involving county business and other matters considered too minor to be heard in state district court. Many are lawyers, although this is not a requirement, and are free to practice law in any manner that does not conflict with their judicial duties. And, as Jackson had learned, they have their hands on the pulse of the community. Very little took place in Post Oak County that he was not aware of.

Sometimes, he wished this were not true. Too often he had been told dark secrets about friends and associates that he would have preferred not to know. Still, he had to admit, this knowledge had, on many occasions, added insight when he had to make tough decisions from the bench.

He was tired when he locked his office and left the courthouse. He had spent the afternoon working on a juvenile case and had ultimately been forced to send young Jordan Spratt to the state school for boys.

The youngster had been caught in a series of minor burglaries. It was a difficult decision. Not that the boy wasn't clearly guilty. There was no doubt about that. But Jackson also knew that Jordan had been abused by his stepfather for years. The law had been helpless to step in and stop it, as the child and his mother had been too terrified of the man to turn him in.

The sun came out that afternoon, and by four the temperature had risen to the fifties. Ice began melting and dripping all over the place. The only reminder of the storm was the dirty slush in the gutters. Jackson began to relax when he turned his car onto Hackberry Street. Giant oak trees shaded the Victorian houses set in wide lawns. The Crain house was at the end of the block. Jackson turned into his driveway and pulled into his carport. He went in through the back porch and walked directly into the kitchen, where he found Lutie Faye Ivory, who took care of Jackson and Patty, already wearing her coat.

"I've got choir practice tonight," she reminded him.

"I remembered," he lied.

"And Patty's still at band practice," she continued. "She called and said she was going home with Ashley for a little while

24

and for you to pick her up there at six."

"Got it."

"Mrs. McBride called. She says for you to call her the minute you get in." She picked up her purse. "There's a big bowl of tuna salad in the fridge. I made you some homemade bread. Y'all eat sandwiches, and I'll fix you a hot lunch tomorrow." Lutie hated it when she had to serve meager meals, but it couldn't be helped. She was the only one in the choir who could sing the high soprano parts.

Jackson retrieved the paper off the hall table and went into his den. He picked up the phone and dialed the McBride number.

"Oh, Jackson." Marlene McBride's voice was breathless. "I had to run to catch the phone. I've been out on the patio with Joe."

"You called?" Jackson was anxious to read his paper.

"Yes, Patty's over here. She said you were picking her up."

"That's what I understand."

"Well, Joe just had the most wonderful idea. He's grilling steaks and we just happen to have one extra because Three decided at the last minute to go off to the coast to talk to a man about a job. We want you to come for dinner. The girls are having hamburgers. So you come on over here right now."

Jackson looked at his watch. Five o'clock. "Five-thirty okay?"

"We'll see you then." She hung up the phone without saying good-bye.

Jackson fixed himself a Scotch and went upstairs to shower and get into a pair of khaki slacks and a polo shirt. He thought about walking the short distance to their house, but in the nick of time remembered that Patty would have her unwieldy French horn with her.

He parked in the McBride driveway, noticing the massive Rice mansion across the street and the little girls playing jump rope on the front sidewalk. He walked up the broad front steps and rang the doorbell.

Marlene opened the door almost immediately and pulled him into the house. Gone was the gaunt look from that day in his office. Today, she wore tailored jeans with a white blouse, her hair, now shining and healthy, was pulled back into a ponytail. She looked every bit as lovely as she had when they were in school together.

"Jackson, I'm so happy," she whispered. "I think all our problems are over."

"How's that?" Jackson kissed her on the cheek.

"Three told his dad that he's taking a job down on the coast. That's miles from here, Jackson. He'll be gone!"

Jackson nodded, hoping this wasn't another false alarm. Three had talked about going to work before. "That's good. Where's Joe?"

"Come on." She led him down the hall to the kitchen. "Let me fix you a drink and you can join him on the deck. Beer? Wine? Tea?"

"Tea sounds good."

He took the drink she handed him and went out the back door, where he found Joe just placing large T-bone steaks on the grill. He closed the lid and motioned toward a pair of lawn chairs.

"Have a seat, buddy." He popped open a beer and took a drink. "How'd you like my new lady barber? Is she something — or what?"

"Something," Jackson said. "What does Marlene have to say about her?"

"She's cool. Marlene knows there's been nobody for me since the day I fell for her." He grinned. "I'm just saying I expect my business to double when word gets around about little Miss Gini."

"You're probably right. She's a good-looking girl."

"Who's that?" Marlene came out carrying a glass of wine.

"Gini," Joe told her. "Some of the guys got a chance to meet her today. Jackson was one of them." He got up to turn the steaks.

"What do you know about her?"

"Only that she's a young mother with a handicapped child. She just walked into the shop one day and asked if I needed any help." He closed the lid on the grill and took a seat next to Marlene.

Marlene smiled fondly at him and turned to Jackson. "How about it, Jackson? Interested?"

Jackson shook his head.

"Still crazy about Mandy?"

"Let's just say I haven't given up on that," he said in a low voice. "But back to Gini. Are you telling me you just hired her off the street?"

"Well, sort of. I let her cut my hair, and she did a damn fine job of it. Right, honey?"

"She did," Marlene confirmed. "Best haircut he's had in a long time."

At that moment, Patty and Ashley came out through the back door.

Jackson smiled at his daughter. She had grown a good three or four inches in the past year, and her hair, once an unruly mop of brown frizz, was now cut short and curled becomingly around her face. She kissed him on the top of his head, obviously glad to see him.

Ashley, wearing jeans and a large man's shirt, smiled shyly at him.

"Ashley's got a boyfriend," Patty teased.

Ashley blushed. "Shut up; I do not."

"Yes, you do." Patty addressed the adults. "Jerry Spratt follows her around everywhere. He's in looove!"

"He's gross!" Ashley said, but with a grin. "I wouldn't be caught dead with him."

"What if he asks you out?" Patty asked.

Jackson stepped in. "Leave her alone," he said. "You're embarrassing her."

"Steaks'll be ready in ten minutes," Joe announced.

Dinner was delicious and Jackson's enjoyment of it was made more so by the knowledge that he could be at home eating tuna salad sandwiches.

Over after-dinner coffee, Jackson brought up the lady barber again.

"Where did she come from?"

"Houston. She worked in a fancy salon there, she said. But she had to deal with stuck-up rich women all day. Gini said they were hard to please and stingy tippers to boot." He put his elbows on the table and leaned forward. "Look, Jackson, she's dependable and damn good at her job. I don't need to know any more."

"True," Jackson admitted. "I just wonder why a woman like that would want to settle in this town."

"I wondered, too, at first," Joe said. "But she says she just feels safer raising her child in a small place."

"She needs a boyfriend," Marlene offered. "Now, who could we find?"

"Leave me out of it," Joe told her. "And Jackson, too."

Both men shook their heads. It was beyond them why women could never leave well enough alone. They always tried to pair people up. Jackson remembered too well the assortment of prospective dates the women in town had paraded before him after Gretchen died. It was only after he made it clear that he was committed to Mandy that they had left him alone.

Marlene got up to refill the coffee cups. "So, Jackson, what is it with you and Mandy? Maybe I can help — talk to her or something."

"I don't think that's a good idea," Jackson said, alarmed. "Mandy's not the kind to be pressured. She'll come around — I hope."

"But what started it?" Marlene pressed. "I thought you-all were the perfect couple."

Jackson didn't want to talk about it. He got to his feet. "It's a school night. I'd better get Patty home. Thanks for dinner."

They were at home before nine. Patty immediately went up to take her bath and Jackson went into his den, thankful finally to light a Don Diego and read the day's news.

Gini McGill sat on the couch in her small apartment on Cypress Street thinking about the fine mess she'd gotten herself into. She'd come to this small town, stumbled on it, really, to escape from one predicament only to find herself in another — different, but just as bad.

It was awful, the lies she'd told. Why had she told Joe Junior she had a child? And a handicapped one, to boot? There was no child, never had been. The closest thing to motherhood she'd ever experienced was the time Jess made her get an abortion. Now, sooner or later, someone was going to expect her to produce a kid.

It was laughable when you thought

about it, her reinventing herself like that. But it was her only chance. Jess would find her, if he wanted to, and when he did, it would not be pleasant. She had been with him long enough to know that he was utterly without scruples — and he didn't like to lose. Her only hope was to change her identity and bury herself in a remote area. That was what she had thought. Now, she wasn't so sure. What if she'd been wrong? What if Jess didn't even care? What if she had screwed up her whole life for nothing?

She got up, made herself a glass of iced tea, and carried it back with her to the couch, thinking of Jess and how the whole thing had started.

She had been trained as a hairdresser and was getting really bored with it. She worked in a Houston salon patronized by wealthy women, which was good for tips but bad for her social life. When she complained to her best friend, Trudy, Trudy had suggested that she apply for massage school.

"It's a short course," Trudy said. "You could get a job at one of the fancy hotels. There you could meet all the guys you want — rich ones."

That was how she'd ended up at the Four Seasons. And Trudy had been right.

There were plenty of men, and they all hit on her. The problem was they were all old, married and fat. Where were all the young, good-looking rich guys? She soon learned that they were all in the hotel gym and racquetball courts — not lying around getting massages.

Then one day, in walked a Greek god wrapped in a towel like the rest of the men. Only his towel wasn't stretched over a big belly and rolls of fat. Her heart pounded when he hiked himself onto the table and sat looking at her, the muscles in his arms and chest hard and glistening in the overhead light. His hair was coal-black and cut to just over the ears. His eyes, also black, seemed to look into her very soul. He had a red, sensuous mouth and an aquiline nose.

Gini smiled, remembering. She had given him the massage of his life, and it had worked. He came back every day for a week. She worked his body until every muscle was jelly — and they talked.

Finally, one day he asked her to go for a drink after work. After one drink, they went up to his room and to bed. After that, she found herself living in a world she had only heard about. He took her places: Cozumel, Las Vegas, New York. It was a magical time. He was up-front about the fact that he was married and intended to stay that way, but by then it didn't matter. She was crazy in love with him. And when he became possessive, she hardly noticed; she thought it was because he loved her.

She had been flattered when he had to know what she did every single minute of the day. It showed he cared. But then the questioning became more intense and then angry. He accused her of seeing other men. But it was not until she discovered she was being followed that she spoke about it. And when she did, he slapped her, hard.

There was one thing she had done right, though, and that was to leave. She was sure of that. She'd seen all those afternoon talk shows, paid attention to what they said about abusive men. If a man hits you once, he'll do it again — and again. Gini was no fool. She began plotting her escape. She went home, unplugged the phone and waited for the black eye and swollen lip to heal. Next, she packed her car and drove north. She would start over somewhere else, somewhere where he'd never find her. She had plenty of time on the road to invent a new life. "Houston in the Rear View Mirror." I've seen that somewhere, she thought. A song? A book?

She had thought when she left Houston that she'd learned her lesson. One married man was enough. Right? Wrong. Now she had fallen head over heels in love with Joe Junior McBride. What a dope she was.

3

Jackson got home from work to find Lutie Faye dropping floured chicken pieces into a cast-iron pot. The smell of the frying made his mouth water. He saw a chocolate cake sitting on the kitchen table with fourteen pink candles in the top.

"Umm, fried chicken," he observed. "And cake, too. What's the occasion?"

"It's Ashley's birthday," she said. "She told her mama she didn't care about any party as long as she could spend the night here and have me cook her some fried chicken."

"Lucky for the rest of us." He grinned. "Where are the girls?"

"You can't hear that racket? They're upstairs playing on those horns." She spat out the last word.

Now he heard it. The sound snaked down the back stairs, assaulting his ears like screeching tires. "Are they getting any better, do you think?"

"Better'n what?" She turned and faced him. "A rooster fight?"

"You're right," he said. "Parenthood has its dark side. Do I have time for a drink and a smoke before dinner?"

"Looky here." She folded her arms and faced him. "Does it look like we're ready to eat? I don't even have the potatoes peeled yet."

"Can I take that for a yes?"

"Get on out of here."

Lutie Faye Ivory was a tiny woman, but full of fire. She had been with them since Patty was a baby, and as far as Jackson and Patty were concerned, she was a member of the family. He winked at her, grinned, and left the room.

Ten minutes later, carrying his drink and the newspaper, he went outside and sat on the porch swing, remembering the old adage, "If you don't like Texas weather, wait a minute." Today had been sunny and warm with only a slight breeze. It was hard to believe that ice had covered the town only two days ago.

He looked out at Hackberry Street from his front porch. It was the scene he had loved since childhood. This house had been built by his grandfather, the first Judge Crain, in 1926. Later, his parents had owned the place; now it was his. He glanced across the street at Ham Boyd's house. Jackson and Ham had played together as boys on the same sidewalks where Patty now rode her bike. He loved the sense of continuity that this place held for him. It was hard for him to imagine why so many people wanted to move away from Post Oak as soon as they grew up. As far as he was concerned, everything he could ever need was right here in this little town.

He might need to do some work on the old place, though. Patty had been begging him to have the house painted.

"It's embarrassing, Daddy," she had said. "The paint's all peeling, and look at how the boards are buckling on the porch. I'm humiliated to have my friends come here."

"Oh, come on. It can't be that bad." Jackson never noticed such things.

"Oh, it is, Daddy. It really is! Can we paint it pink? I saw one in a movie that was pink. It was awesome. And then can we do something about the drapes in the living room? They've actually got rips in them. And we need to paint the inside, too. The wallpaper's hanging down in the hall."

Jackson had checked and found that she was right. His grandmother's silk draperies had rotted away in spots. And he was sure they hadn't been this grayish color when he was a boy. And the wallpaper did seem to be coming loose in spots. He would have to get somebody in to look at the place. He wouldn't know where to start.

After supper, the girls walked down to the convenience store for Slushes and Jackson took his newspaper into the den. The old house was quiet for a change. He sank into his leather chair by the hearth and, with a sigh of deep contentment, lit a Don Diego and watched the smoke coil into the lamplight. He had read the front page and was just turning to the sports section when the phone rang.

It was the sheriff. "Judge, Leonard Gibbs here. You tied up?"

"No, why?"

"Bad business," the sheriff replied. "Joe Junior McBride's been murdered."

Ten minutes later, Jackson pulled his car into the driveway of the McBride house, a prairie-style, built in the 1920s. As he made his way up the sidewalk toward the front door, he noticed an older model Ford Thunderbird resting on blocks in the driveway. The hood was up and a red mechanic's rag had been left on the front fender. Tools lay scattered about. Probably one of Three's projects, he thought.

Dooley Burns, the sheriff's deputy, stood guard just inside. "Go on in, Judge." He pointed toward the den down the hall. Dooley lowered his voice. "Shit if it ain't a mess in there."

When Jackson entered the den, he saw that Dooley had been right. Chairs were overturned, pictures torn from the walls and tossed around the floor, and the coffee-table top had been smashed, leaving shards of glass glittering on the floor. A brownish stain spread from the still figure on the couch across the dull green carpet.

Jackson strode over to the couch and stood looking down. His stomach churned.

"Where's Marlene?" he asked, his jaw set.

The sheriff pointed. Marlene was sitting in a wing back chair in the shadows at the opposite end of the room. Jackson crossed the room to her and looked down. The red sleeveless blouse and white Capri pants she wore were wrinkled and splotched with dark stains. Her glorious hair hung limply around her ashen face. She looked at him without emotion, but he saw that her eyes were dilated and her hands shook as she twisted the balled-up tissue in her lap. He knelt in front of her, and she leaned into his arms, still as a corpse. She didn't speak.

Jackson held her for a moment, then turned to the deputy, who had entered the room behind him. "Is the ambulance on its way?"

"S'posed to be," Dooley drawled. "I called them soon as we got here."

"Well, call them again," Jackson snapped. "Tell them to hurry. Mrs. McBride is in shock."

He gently settled Marlene back in her chair, then spotting an afghan on the floor, tucked it around her body. "Stay still, honey," he whispered. "They'll be here shortly."

Jackson turned to the sheriff. "What have you got?"

"Right now it looks like an intruder, Judge, what with this mess and all. I've called in the crime scene team from Eastlake. We'll know more when they get here."

Jackson bent over the still figure on the couch. Joe Junior lay on his side, facing the back. At first glance, he appeared to be napping, but leaning in closer, Jackson could see the red gash that laid open his throat from ear to ear. Blood had soaked the couch around him and splattered the wall behind it. Jackson's nostrils flared at the sweet, metallic scent of it.

Just then, the EMS crew arrived. Jackson addressed the tall black woman who entered first, followed by a blond young man. "Take care of Mrs. McBride first, Amy. She's in shock." The woman immediately turned to Marlene and began her work. Amy Tubbs was good. Jackson was glad to see she was on this job.

"Judge, there's something I want you to see," the sheriff said.

Jackson followed him out of the room and to the short hall that led from the kitchen to the garage. A washer and dryer stood beneath two windows along one wall. One of the windows was open. The sheriff pointed. Blood smears marred the white porcelain fixtures. Through the open window, Jackson could see that the screen had an L-shaped cut large enough for a man to pass through.

Jackson nodded. "Have you checked outside?"

"Not yet."

"For God's sake, man, why not?"

The sheriff looked sheepish. "Well, Judge, I didn't like leaving Mrs. McBride alone, so I sent Dooley out while I waited for you to get here." The sheriff took a flashlight off his belt. "I guess we'd better do it now."

Jackson picked up a dish towel from the pile of clothes on the floor and, covering his hand, switched on the garage light. "Let's go."

The moon was full, affording a good view of the ground as they walked around the side of the garage to the backyard. The sheriff directed the beam of his flashlight toward the soft ground just under the window where someone had prepared a planting area. He walked over and bent down to examine the spot.

"Something's mighty strange about this, Judge. Come take a look."

Jackson came and stood beside the sheriff. "I don't see . . . wait a minute . . . of course. There aren't any footprints."

"Maybe the guy jumped over the bed." The sheriff scratched his head.

"Possible," Jackson said. "But if this is the way he got in, he would have had to stand right here in this spot. And aren't those footprints in the dew leading out toward the alley?"

"Seem to be." Sheriff Gibbs trained the light toward the lawn. A worn path in the grass led from the back door to a clothesline that stretched across the back of the yard. The footprints cut an angle from the house toward a gate in the privacy fence that led to the alley. The two men walked toward the gate, avoiding the prints in the grass. The glow from a halogen security light in a neighbor's yard illuminated the alley. Two garbage cans, overflowing, stood just outside the fence.

"See any more prints, Judge?" the sheriff asked.

"No, not on this asphalt, but shine your light down that way." He pointed. "It looks like there's something . . ."

"By God, it's a wallet." Using his handkerchief, the sheriff picked up the object, elaborately tooled with Western motifs, and using the light, opened it to examine its contents. "Empty. This thing is so beat up, it could have fallen out of somebody's trash."

Jackson reached for the wallet and recognized it immediately. "It's Joe Junior's, all right, and he didn't throw it away. Somebody dropped it here tonight."

Joe Junior had taken pride in this wallet because Three had made it for him at Boy Scout camp when he was twelve. Intricately tooled with Western motifs, it was laced together with leather thongs. Jackson remembered Joe Junior taking it to a leather shop to be relaced when the original thongs had worn out.

The sheriff beamed the flashlight down the alley and along the fence lines on either side. "Looks like that's all we're gonna find out here. Plain to see we've got a robbery as well as a murder on our hands."

Jackson nodded and the two men turned and walked back toward the house. "Thing I can't understand is, how come there's no footprints in that flower bed under the window."

Jackson shook his head. He was wondering the same thing.

When they got back inside, the crime lab team from Eastlake had arrived. Jackson noticed that Marlene was no longer in the room. He went looking for her. As he started down the hall toward the bedroom wing, he saw Amy Tubbs coming out of one of the rooms.

"I've given her a sedative," she said. "She's resting. Judge Crain, I called Mae Applewaite to come over and stay with her tonight. She ought to be here shortly. And knowing Mrs. Applewaite, she'll mobilize all the church ladies to take charge. Mrs. McBride keeps asking about Ashley. Do you happen to know where she is?"

"She's spending the night with Patty," Jackson said. "I'll tell her what's happened when I get home, and then, unless Marlene needs her here, I'll just let her stay."

"Good idea. I'll see you, Judge. You take care now."

"Oh, Amy, one more thing. Who called 911?"

"It was Brother Steve Largent, I believe."

Steve lived across the street in the Rice mansion. Jackson wondered why he had not stayed around until the EMS arrived, but that could wait. He pushed open the door to the bedroom. The room was dark except for a nightlight over the bedside table. Marlene lay on a large canopied bed with her eyes closed. Jackson started to back out the door when she spoke. "I'm not asleep. Come and sit with me for a few minutes."

Jackson entered the room and sat on the edge of the bed, taking Marlene's hand in his. "You should sleep," he said.

"I have to say something to you, Jackson. It's important."

Jackson waited.

"It's about the time I came to you talking divorce. Jackson, I didn't mean that. I'd never leave Joe . . . or hurt him."

"Of course not, honey. Don't even think about that."

"Jackson, you know that I'd never hurt Joe, don't you?"

Jackson was surprised. "You think you're a suspect? Not a chance. Nobody thinks you had anything to do with this thing. You're just upset. Your mind's playing tricks."

Marlene took a deep breath and expelled it slowly. "You think so? Because I didn't . . . I couldn't . . ." Her speech was becoming slurred.

"Of course not."

She closed her eyes, and Jackson waited until her breathing slowed to an even pace. He then extracted his hand from hers and started to rise from the bed. She reached for his hand and grasped it tightly, her eyes now fully open. "Ashley. Where's my baby?"

"She's at my house. Don't worry. She can stay as long as she likes." He stood. "Get some rest. I'll see you tomorrow."

Just then, there was a tap on the door and an agitated voice called from the hall. "Marlene. It's Gerry. Can I come in?"

Jackson recognized Gerald McBride's voice. He was band director at Patty's school as well as being Joe Junior's adoptive brother.

Jackson looked inquiringly at Marlene, and at her nod, opened the door to admit him. "My God, I just found out. Marlene,

47

honey, are you all right?" He rushed into the room and stood looking down at her.

"All right?" A note of hysteria crept into her voice. "The only man I ever loved is lying dead with his . . ." She turned and faced the wall.

A look Jackson couldn't read flashed across Gerald McBride's face. It disappeared as quickly as it had come as he rushed to her side. Taking Jackson's place by the bed, he took her hand. "I'm so sorry."

"Where were you, Gerry?" She still faced the wall.

"Dearest, I told you when I left that I was going to marching practice. I'd left my cell phone in the band hall, so I didn't get the message until practice was over."

"You were here earlier?" Jackson asked.

"Just for a minute," the band director said. "I had dropped by to leave some music for Ashley — but then I remembered she was spending the night at your house, Jackson, so I took it to practice with me."

"What time was that?" Jackson asked.

"Around six. Why?"

"It's a murder investigation. See or hear anything out of the ordinary?"

Gerald thought a minute. "No . . . no, I

guess not. The only odd thing was that Junior was stretched out on the couch watching the news. He's usually in his La-Z-Boy. Marlene was in the kitchen putting up the supper things, so I went in and chatted with her for a few minutes. She finished up and went upstairs to take a shower and I left. That must have been around six-twenty. What happened here, Jackson?"

Jackson, speaking rapidly, told him the facts. "It looks like an intruder got in while Marlene was upstairs. Maybe Joe woke up and caught him in the act. That's just a guess. We'll know more tomorrow when we get the report from the crime scene crew." He opened the door. "I'm going to talk to Steve Largent. Mae Applewaite will be here any minute to stay with Marlene. Can you wait until she gets here?"

"Of course." Gerald patted Marlene's shoulder. "I'll be here as long as she needs me."

Jackson left his car parked where it was and walked across the street to the Rice mansion. The little girls he'd seen days before were nowhere in sight. Now the large terraced yard was deserted. When he mounted the wide front steps and crossed to the door, he heard the normal commotion that comes when a house is full of children — footsteps running, young voices raised to be heard over the television and, in the game room, the clatter of pool cues striking balls. He rang the bell and prayed he'd be heard over the noise. After waiting a moment, he rang again, listening for the sound of approaching footsteps. After the third try, he pushed open the door and went into the wide front hall.

A massive stairway set ten feet back divided the hall. Above his head, a gigantic brass chandelier flooded the room with light. A teenaged boy he recognized as being one of Patty's classmates came out of the parlor to the left.

"Hi, Brad," Jackson said. "See Brother Steve?"

Steve Largent, although not now an acting pastor, was an ordained Baptist minister.

"Oh, hey, Judge," the boy said. "He's back in the kitchen. Want me to get him for you?"

"Thanks, I'll find him." Jackson walked past the staircase and down the hall toward the rear of the house. He found Steve and his pretty wife, Vanessa, sitting at the kitchen table drinking coffee and talking softly. Their faces were solemn.

Jackson admired Steve. He was a master

at people skills and had been the best preacher the local church had ever had, gladly giving of himself to the lives of his flock. The congregation had been shocked when he announced that he was quitting his job and, with Vanessa, was opening a home for displaced children. It was simply a ministry of a different kind, he told them. And it had worked. The couple had used Vanessa's inheritance money to buy the old Rice place, which was now home to an ever-changing number of kids of all colors and ages.

The couple jumped to their feet when Jackson entered the room.

"Jackson," Vanessa said, "we saw your car at the McBrides'. How is Marlene? Can I help?"

"She's been given a sedative." Jackson gratefully accepted the mug of coffee she placed in his hands. He sank into a chair, suddenly very tired.

"What do you know?" The preacher's face showed concern.

"Nothing yet." Jackson sipped his coffee. "I was hoping you might shed some light. Amy Tubbs said it was you who called the EMS."

"That's right," Steve answered. "I happened to stop by to return Joe's pipe wrench. Apparently, Marlene had just come downstairs and found him. She was hysterical. I called the ambulance — I guess they notified Sheriff Gibbs."

"Why did you leave?" Jackson was surprised that he hadn't waited for the paramedics to get there.

"I sure didn't want to." His brow furrowed. "But Marlene insisted on sitting in the room with Joe to wait. I didn't try to stop her; it would have only upset her more."

Jackson nodded.

"But it was obvious that that room was a crime scene. Everyone nowadays knows that you don't contaminate a crime scene."

"Right," Jackson said. "So, what did you do?"

"Waited in the hall until Sheriff Gibbs got there. He told me to go on home and wait, that he'd be wanting to talk to me later. Jackson, I really didn't feel good about leaving, but the sheriff insisted."

"Jackson, did Marlene see who did it?" Vanessa asked.

"As far as we know, she was upstairs taking a shower," Jackson said. "Did the two of you see, or hear, anything unusual?"

"Umm . . . not unusual, maybe, but I saw Three backing out of the driveway in that new truck of his," Vanessa said. She laughed self-consciously. "Well, duh, he lives there. How unusual can that be?"

"He was burning rubber," Steve commented. "That's what makes it unusual. He really treats that truck well."

"Interesting," Jackson said. "I thought he was out of town. Anything else?"

The two thought a moment. "There is one thing," Vanessa said slowly. "I don't know whether I should mention it. Sounds like I'm gossiping, you know? Anyway, it's probably nothing."

Jackson waited.

"Well, it's just that I saw the new lady barber driving past the house earlier."

"Maybe she lives down that way, honey," Steve said.

"Could be," Vanessa said. "But Mae told me she lived on the other side of town — in those Fireside Apartments." She looked at Jackson. "I don't know how Mae finds out, but she knows everything about everybody."

The pastor smiled. "I know. She gets it down at that Knitter's Nook. Those ladies don't miss a thing."

Jackson had to agree. At one time or another, most of the women in town had occasion to visit the Knitter's Nook, run by

Jane and Esther Archer. A vast amount of information was heard and passed on through those doors.

Vanessa shrugged. "Well, anyway, that's not the first time we've seen her. Sometimes at night, she drives really slow past their house."

Jackson drained his coffee mug and got to his feet. "You've been helpful," he said. "Keep an eye on Marlene, will you? And if you think of anything else, let me or the sheriff know."

"Will do." Steve walked Jackson to the door. "How's Ashley? We could have her over here . . ."

"Not necessary," Jackson said. "She's with Patty at my house."

He got into his car and started the engine, dreading the task of telling Ashley.

4

When Jackson got home, he found Patty and Ashley huddled over the computer in the den. They were giggling at something on the screen, but their smiles quickly faded when they saw the look on Jackson's face. As gently as he knew how, he told them what had happened at the McBride house.

Ashley's eyes grew wide with horror, and she burst into tears. Instinctively, Jackson crossed the room and took the girl in his arms. He held her while she sobbed. Patty, not knowing what to do, reached for a tissue from the box on the computer table and handed it to Ashley. When the worst of the crying was over, Jackson gently led her to the couch and eased her down onto it.

"My mom . . . is she okay?"

The truth was the only way to go, Jackson thought. "Well, your mom's awfully upset. They've given her a shot to calm her down, and she was sleeping when I left."

"Is she there alone? I'd better go home

in case she wakes up."

"She's not alone. Gerald is there with her, and Mae Applewaite is going to come over and stay. Honey, we want you to stay with us for a few days." He handed her a fresh tissue. "I talked to your mom about it, and she agreed it would be best. She won't be worrying about you if you're here with us."

"Where's Three?"

Jackson's jaw set. "We don't know exactly. He was supposed to go fishing somewhere, I think. But, back to you, do you agree to stay here with us?"

"Okay, I guess, if my mom wants me to." She blew her nose on the tissue. "But can I go see her?"

"Of course you can, but tomorrow. Tonight, I want you to try your best to get some rest and put it out of your mind if you can."

After asking a few more questions which Jackson answered as honestly as he could, the girls went upstairs.

Jackson made himself a Scotch and stood at the window, sipping his drink and looking at the moonlight falling on the still, green lawns of his neighbors. In the distance a dog barked and he heard the whistle of a train. It was hard to believe that only a few blocks away, a brutal murder had occurred.

Jackson had lived in Post Oak all his life except for the time he had been away to attend college at the University of Texas in Austin and later, UT Law School. His father, also Judge Crain (because of the one term he had served as a state district judge), had expected him to enter his lucrative corporate law practice, but Jackson had had other ideas. Interested in police work from childhood, he had applied to join the FBI, but was turned down because of less than perfect eyesight. He had returned home to Post Oak. Although he was disappointed at being turned down by the feds, he was determined to follow his interest in the criminal side of things. He served two terms as DA before going into private practice. It was only four years ago that the town fathers had approached him to run for county judge. Soon after he took office, his wife, Gretchen, was diagnosed with leukemia. She died a year later. When Gretchen died and he was left to raise Patty alone, he knew the travel and uncertainty of his criminal practice had to come to an end. Surprisingly, Jackson discovered that he enjoyed the judicial side of the law, and the regular hours made it easier to care for a girl just entering her teens.

The romantic side of Jackson's life had been nonexistent until a year ago, when Mandy d'Alejandro appeared in town. She had been sent by the State Historical Commission to manage the town's Main Street Project. This was a designation given certain towns across the state. It was a boon for rural areas as it brought with it the funds and expertise needed to revitalize selected small towns in Texas before they were devoured by the hungry metropolitan areas. Unfortunately, the Main Street Project had been more successful than Jackson's pursuit of Mandy. Due to a misunderstanding, she was keeping him at arm's length, and Jackson was at a loss to know what to do about it.

His mind was drawn back to the scene in the McBride living room. Something was niggling in the back of his mind about that scene; something was not right. He strained to grasp what it was, but the answer eluded him. He drained his glass and set it on the table, and turning off the lamp, went up to bed. Maybe it would come to him during the night.

The next morning he called the sheriff from his office in the courthouse.

"He's asleep, Judge." It was the sheriff's

58

wife, Norma Jean. "I'll wake him up, if you want me to, but he didn't get to bed until after three."

"No, just tell him to call me later." Jackson hung up the phone and dialed Mandy's number. He felt the usual thrill when he heard her soft, slightly accented voice.

"Hi." He knew she'd recognize his voice.

"Oh, Jackson . . ."

"How are you?"

"I'm fine. Jackson, I just heard about Joe Junior. It's too awful. I know he was your friend."

"Yeah, it was bad and I'm mad as hell. He was one of my oldest friends, you know."

"I'm so sorry."

"Mandy, I was wondering if you'd have lunch with me." He felt only slightly guilty about playing the sympathy card.

"Well . . . I guess so. We'll have to go at eleven-thirty, though. I have a twelve forty-five appointment."

"Good. I'll pick you up. Pembrooke House okay?"

"Sure. My other line's ringing. I'll see you then."

As Jackson was hanging up the phone, his secretary, Edna Buchannan, poked her head in the door. "You free?"

"Sure." Jackson glanced up at Edna and motioned for her to take a seat in the red leather client's chair in front of his desk. "Got something on your mind?"

"Damn straight I do." She nodded her over-permed head emphatically. Edna was Jackson's age but looked older, partly due to her firm belief that you couldn't use too much lipstick, pancake makeup and Maybelline mascara, velvet black. By mid-morning the makeup had cracked around her laugh lines and the lipstick had crept up into the vertical lines around her lips that years of smoking Virginia Slims had etched there. She pulled a crumpled pack from her skirt pocket, extracted a cigarette, and lit up. "You wouldn't believe what that son of a bitch has gone and got us into now."

Jackson sighed. Edna's problems almost always involved the latest scheme her husband, Orville, had hatched up.

"He's out in the backyard this very minute making a mess like you wouldn't believe."

"Doing what?" Jackson knew there was no point in trying to rush Edna once she had a full head of steam going.

"Building cages. He's already got five of

'm built. Says he needs at least a dozen, which, as you well know having been in my backyard, ain't even gonna leave room for Little Orvie's swing set. Little bitty cages no more 'n five feet square. He's got a big old roll of hog-wire fencin' out there and he's settin' PVC posts right smack in the middle of my vegetable plot." Edna took a long drag from her cigarette and exhaled an amazing plume of smoke.

Jackson nodded.

"And you oughta see what he's done in my garden shed, Jackson. He's put in a sink and a big old table — and I caught him sneaking out of the house with my hair dryer and my best Vidal Sassoon styling brush."

Jackson was intrigued in spite of himself. "You have electricity in your garden shed?"

"Naw. Leastways we didn't. Now he's gone and taken that real long orange extension cord off the weed smacker and plugged it in on the back porch where the washing machine is."

"Well, Edna, what the hell is he doing?"

Edna fairly shook with indignation. "He's plannin' on opening a goddam dog kennel with a goddam grooming business. I can just see it now, dogs barking at all hours of the day and night, neighbors complainin', folks driving up and down my driveway and trompin' through my flower beds. It ain't enough that I have to put up with his old momma criticizing everything I do, and tryin' to lord it over me just because she's town and my folks come from out at Sugar Hill, now there's this. I ain't gonna take it anymore, Jackson. I just plain can't!"

To Jackson's dismay, she burst into tears. He handed her a tissue from the box on his desk. He thought a minute while she composed herself. "Here's something we could do," he said. "I'll bet Orville never thought to get a license to open a business. We could probably turn him in to city hall . . . or there might be some sort of zoning ordinance on your street. Isn't your house in the historical district?"

Edna put up her hand. "Hell, Jackson." She blew her nose loudly. "You men are all alike. I didn't say I wanted you to do anything about it. I just needed to get it off my chest."

Jackson shook his head. "Fine. Then could we get some work done this morning?"

"Jackson, how come you didn't tell me about Joe Junior gettin' murdered?"

"And when was I supposed to do that?

Between the weed smacker and the Vidal Sassoon styling brush?"

Edna grinned, feeling better since she'd unburdened herself. "Go to hell," she said.

Jackson shook his head and picked up the phone. Sometimes he thought Edna was more trouble than she was worth; other times he wondered how he'd ever gotten along without her. She was amazingly efficient in spite of her eccentricities.

Sheriff Leonard J. Gibbs had been up late last night going over the evidence in the McBride case with the crime scene investigators. He'd slept late and then had been called out early that morning to work a wreck involving an eighteen-wheeler and a Toyota out on Highway 11. At ten-thirty, he was finally sitting down to breakfast in his quarters adjoining the jail.

Of medium height with a red face and a substantial bay window, Sheriff Gibbs often wondered how he'd been so lucky as to have married the lovely Norma Jean Beazley, who had been head drum majorette and most popular girl in high school. Of course, the sheriff had to admit, he hadn't been so bad back then either, being captain of the football team and all. Norma Jean had put on a few pounds herself, and her blond curls had faded some, but her eyes were still wide and blue, and they hadn't lost their sparkle. Now she set a plate of scrambled eggs and sausage in front of him.

"More coffee, Shug?"

"Um-hmm."

The sheriff was glancing through the paper.

"Oh, I forgot to tell you, Horace Kinkaid called while you were out. He wants a story about the murder."

"Course he does." The sheriff polished off his coffee and folded the paper just as someone knocked at the large metal door that separated the living quarters from the jail proper.

Norma started toward the door but the sheriff, moving quickly, beat her there. He couldn't seem to get it through Norma Jean's head that you couldn't just open the jailhouse door to anybody who happened to knock the way she could when they still lived on the farm. He placed his eye over the peephole, and seeing it was Jackson Crain, swung the door open wide.

"Come on in, Judge. Coffee?"

When Jackson nodded, Norma retreated to the kitchen and came back holding a full mug.

"Let's go in my office. Those crime scene folks came up with some damned odd findings."

"Where's Dooley?" Jackson asked.

"He's out directing traffic around a wrecked semi out on Highway 11. Thing turned over right smack across the road. Luckily it wasn't nothing but a milk truck. It's a damned mess, but nothing hazardous."

"Anybody hurt?"

"They had to take the Cooley kid to the hospital for a few scratches, but he ain't hurt bad. Lucky, too. The little bastard ran a stop sign and the trucker had to swerve to keep from hitting him. The truck jackknifed and the kid ended up in a ditch. His daddy ain't likely to be too pleased about what that's going to do to his insurance, though."

"So, what did the crime scene guys find out last night?"

The sheriff pulled a yellow folder from the stack on his old rolltop desk. He took out several sheets of paper stapled together and handed them to Jackson. "Read this and tell me what you think."

Jackson read through the papers quickly, then turned back and reread the first few pages. He frowned. "Bloodstains in the hall bathroom sink? Is that downstairs?"

"Yeah. It's the one Ashley and Three use. Marlene and him had a master bath off their bedroom. Whoever did it had tried to wash the blood down the drain. But, you know, Luminol showed it right up, clear as day."

"Any prints?"

"They're analyzing that right now."

Jackson nodded. "And what's this about Joe's driver's license and credit cards? They found them? Where?"

"They were hid way back in the junk drawer in the kitchen — by the telephone. You know the junk drawer. Everybody's got one."

"Yeah." Jackson was still studying the report. "So, what do you think, Sheriff?"

"Same thing as you're thinking, I guess."

"Inside job?"

"It's looking that way." The sheriff folded his arms over his belly. "We're still trying to get hold of Three. He was supposed to be in Rockport fishing, as you know, but nobody down there remembers seeing him."

Jackson looked at his watch. Eleven-fifteen. "I've got to get going. Let me know when they find Three."

After Jackson left, the sheriff leaned back

in his swivel chair and studied the report for the third time, hoping to find something that would refute the obvious scenario: that Joe Junior had been murdered by someone with a legitimate reason for being in that house. As far as he could see, that would point to either Marlene or Three, who was supposedly out of town. Ashley, he crossed off the list. She had been with the judge's daughter for the whole evening. Of course, Gerald McBride had been at the house, too. But if Marlene was to be believed, he had been with her the whole time. That left only one person in the family with no alibi, and Sheriff Gibbs did not want to think that Marlene McBride had done this. Still, he was aware that she had had to put up with a lot in that marriage. Joe Junior's coddling of his no-good son at the expense of Marlene's daughter was common gossip around town. But he couldn't eliminate Gerald. It was also common knowledge that he was in love with Marlene and had been since school days. The sheriff also knew that the man was equally as devoted to his brother. He would never try to steal Joe's wife even if that had been possible. Could he have snapped? It was something to think about. He frowned and picked up the telephone.

He needed to find Three — and the sooner the better.

A short time later, Jackson, with Mandy seated beside him, pulled into the shaded driveway of a restored Victorian house. The Pembrooke House was a bed-and-breakfast run by Annabeth Jones and her single son, John B. To add to their income, they served lunch on weekdays. Although the selections were limited, the food was excellent. It was prepared by John B, who had recently graduated from Le Gourmet, a chef's college in nearby Texarkana.

They entered the house through a painted arbor covered with climbing roses. Annabeth stood behind an antique counter opposite the front door. When she saw Jackson and Mandy, she came around the counter with outstretched arms.

"My two favorite people in the whole world," she cooed. "Come give me a big hug."

Jackson caught the knowing twinkle in her eyes and knew that this lunch date would be broadcast to every interested ear in Post Oak before they were even finished with their salads.

"Come on, you two." Annabeth picked up two large white menus. "I'm taking you to the best table in the house."

Jackson winked at Mandy as they followed Annabeth into the dining room, which thankfully held only a few early customers. Jackson knew from experience that every table would be taken by noon.

Annabeth led them to a table for two at the rear of the room. It was in a small alcove surrounded on three sides by windows. "Enjoy your meal," she said. "I'll go get your water while you decide what to eat. I do recommend the Crèpes Newburg. John B uses sherry in the sauce and those little bitty mushrooms. They are just too divine!" She hurried off to fetch their water.

Jackson grinned at Mandy. "Sorry you came?"

Mandy smiled back. "Not a bit. I've been in this town long enough to know that seeing us together again would give the ladies something to talk about."

"And you don't mind?"

"Jackson, if I minded I wouldn't be here. What are you having?"

"I think the trout," Jackson said, "and a cup of corn chowder. You?"

"I'll have the crèpes. Can't disappoint John B." She folded her menu and placed it on the table beside her.

Jackson watched her. Even a gesture as simple as discarding a menu took on a special grace when Mandy did it. Her hands, honey-colored and delicate, reminded him of a fine porcelain figurine his mother had once owned. And yet he knew she was not at all likely to shatter the way his mother's Dresden piece had done when, as a boy, he had smashed it with a baseball. Mandy had an inner core of strength that attracted him even more than her outward appearance of vulnerability. Her hair, dark and full, was pulled back with a clip, setting off her wide forehead, huge brown eyes, and generous mouth. Taken individually, her features might have been ordinary, but in combination Jackson found them captivating.

"Jackson, stop looking at me like that."

"Okay." He picked up his spoon and went to work on his soup. "If you promise me something."

She looked wary. "What?"

"That you'll give me another chance."

"Jackson, I thought we had that settled."

"You did; not me."

Jackson thought back to a year ago, when his sister-in-law, Dora, had been murdered. On a trip to south Texas, Jackson had inadvertently stumbled on a piece of information about Mandy's family.

70

When he had been forced to go public with the knowledge, Mandy had taken offense and accused him of spying on her. No matter how hard he tried, Jackson had been unable to convince her that he had gone to her home town for no other reason than to investigate a murder. After the initial blow-up, they had settled into an uneasy civility. Jackson had tried dating other women, but with little success. He couldn't get Mandy out of his mind. Today he felt encouraged. This was the first time he had been able to persuade her to go out with him.

He decided to forge ahead. "Mandy, would —"

"Tell me about Joe Junior." She took a bite of roll and chewed it while she waited for an answer.

Jackson got the message. "Someone slit his throat with a razor while he slept on the couch." He decided not to mention the findings of the crime scene investigators just yet. "Could have been an intruder."

"Umm. How is Marlene?"

"Fragile. I just hope she can hold up."

"She has to, Jackson. She has a child to consider."

Jackson knew Mandy would be able to handle the situation, no matter how heartbreaking. Marlene was another matter. She had always been vulnerable.

"Ashley's staying with us for a while." He put down his fork. "They haven't found Three yet. He's supposed to be in Rockport fishing."

"Really? I could have sworn . . . well, maybe I was wrong."

"What?"

"Nothing, I guess. It's just that last night, I had to go to the Super Save for milk. It was about ten. I could have sworn I saw him drive by as I was getting into my car."

"What was he driving?"

"That brand-new truck his papa bought him. A duelly? Is that what they call them? Bright green."

"I'll tell the sheriff," Jackson said. "Are you going to have time for dessert?"

"No. I'll have to get back, pretty soon, Jackson. It's been fun seeing you, though."

"Enough fun to make you want to go to the country club fish fry with me?"

She looked at him. "Jackson, I don't . . . well, when is it?"

"Saturday night."

"I'll think about it. Okay? Call me on Thursday."

5

When Jackson got back to his office, two calls waited for him. Edna stood by his desk holding the pink message slips.

"The sheriff says there's nothing new, but he'd like to talk to you, and could you stop by the jail when you can. He'd come here, but Norma Jean's getting her hair done and he can't leave."

Jackson nodded. "What else?"

"This one's kind of funny. Old Lady Rice called. Says she's got to see you this afternoon."

"Don't call her Old Lady Rice," Jackson said, irritated.

"Why not? She's old — and she's sure as hell a lady."

Jackson gave up. "Did she say what she wanted?"

"Nope. Want some coffee?"

Jackson shook his head. "I'd better go find out what the sheriff's got on his mind. I'll be back by three."

Jackson was fond of the portly sheriff. A man in his sixties, he had been a rancher all his life. When the price of cattle had taken a nose dive several years ago, he had run for sheriff as a means to hold on to his acreage, and because of his popularity, had been elected. He was as surprised as anyone to find out he had a flair for law enforcement. He was tough on law-breakers, but at all times fair.

The sheriff was sitting with his boots propped on the desk staring out the window when Jackson walked in.

"You wanted to see me?" Jackson asked.

Sheriff Gibbs took his feet down and pushed his hair back from his face. "Yeah, Judge, I do," he said. "I hate like hell to say it, but I'm thinking we're dealing with an inside job on this McBride murder."

Jackson nodded and waited for him to continue.

"Luminol showed bloodstains all over the sink in the downstairs bath and on the carpet in the hall. It was on the linoleum in the kitchen and laundry room, too. Course, somebody'd tried to clean it up, but didn't do a very good job."

Jackson thought about this. "What about that wallet in the alley?"

"A ruse." The sheriff picked up a pack of cigarettes from the desk, looked at it and put it back again. "The crime scene guys used the Luminol on the yard, too. Traces of blood going out to the alley and back to the house is all they found. If the feller had been running off, we'd've had more blood going on down the alley. See what I mean?"

Jackson's brow furrowed. He didn't want it to be a family member. "Couldn't it have rubbed off their shoes after a time?" he asked.

"Well, yeah, of course. And it did get fainter, but the thing was, that was going back to the house — the back door, to be exact."

"I'm sorry to hear that," Jackson said.

"Me, too." He picked up the cigarettes again, shook one out and lit it. "Trying to quit," he said. "See, the thing is, that Luminol is powerful stuff. If the killer had run off down that alley, those guys would have found something — even a little bitty drop shows up."

Jackson digested this information before he spoke. "What do you know about Joe's helper, the lady barber?"

"Nothing, why?"

Jackson told him what Vanessa had told him. "Van says she makes a habit of driving by the house."

"Well, now, let's think about that a

75

minute," the sheriff said. "Where could she be headed to that's out past that street?"

"The lake," Jackson said. "That street runs into Highway Nine, and that leads to the lake."

"And what's at the lake that a young woman would want to go to after dark?"

"The Broken Oar," Jackson said.

"Bingo. It ain't the classiest place in town, but it's for sure the only place. Maybe she gets lonesome and wants a little action. No law against that."

"No, I guess not," Jackson admitted. "But that still doesn't explain why she was driving so slow past Joe's house. Would you run a check on her, just in case?"

The sheriff was still doubtful. "I could, but, Judge, like I said, the evidence is still going to point to someone in that house."

"I know." Jackson unwrapped a Don Diego and reached for the sheriff's lighter. "But, just for the sake of argument, suppose Joe was having a fling with her, and suppose she took it more seriously than he did . . ."

"Judge, now that ain't Joe, and you know it."

"Yeah, you're right," Jackson said. "But would you check her out anyway? I've just got a hunch on this."

"Sure, Judge, if you want me to. I should have something for you late this afternoon."

Back at his desk, Jackson waited for Myrtice Rice. What could she possibly want from him? The Rices had been an institution in Post Oak for as long as Jackson could remember. At one time extremely wealthy, the couple had built the old Rice mansion back in the thirties. Ray Rice had lost his money, nobody knew how or when, because they had put on a show of wealth long after the money was gone. They now lived on Ray's meager Social Security check. Two years ago, they had been in danger of losing the house. That was when Vanessa and Steve had gotten the idea of opening a children's home. They had purchased the house but insisted that the Rices stay on. As far as Jackson could tell, it was a happy arrangement. Vanessa told everybody that Myrtice and Ray were irreplaceable.

"They're the kind of grandparents these kids never knew," she was fond of saying.

Myrtice was a small woman, birdlike in her mannerisms. Her snow-white hair was a cap of tight curls. Jackson had to smile as she sat primly in front of him, feet crossed at the ankles and holding a large black handbag in her lap. Her china-blue eyes regarded him levelly.

"Now, Mr. Crain, I knew your mother and grandmother, and I'm counting on you to help me."

"I'll do anything I can," Jackson said. "Why don't you tell me about it?"

"I want to make a will," she said. "And I need it right away. There's no time to waste, Mr. Crain. I want a joint will for Ray and myself."

"Mrs. Rice, I'm sure you already have a will. Didn't my father write one for you?"

Jackson's father had been the Rice's attorney before he died.

"Yes, of course," she said. "But that was back when Ray had money." She dug into her purse and produced the will. "It's no good now."

Jackson took the document and glanced through it. "Well, of course there is a lot in here that no longer applies. But, Mrs. Rice, if one of you dies, the survivor would still receive the other's share."

She leaned forward. "Mr. Crain, you still don't know all the facts. Can I count on your discretion?"

Jackson hid a smile. "Of course."

"I want to make it so Ray can't get his hands on any of it. I want to give everything we have to Vanessa and Steve — for the children, you know."

"Why not to each other? Then the last to die could leave it to the home."

"No!" She shook her head until her curls bobbed. "It has to be like this. You see" — she lowered her voice — "Ray's not himself anymore."

"How is that?"

"Mr. Crain, it's not anything I can pinpoint, just a certain look in his eyes sometimes. I've been married to the man for sixty-three years. I know him inside and out. Now, if he gets his hands on any money, he's bound to spend it foolishly."

"Maybe his doctor could . . ."

"Mr. Crain! Are you going to help me, or are you not?"

"Well," Jackson said, "we could set up a trust with the Largents as overseers. That way, you could both be taken care of, and the rest could go to them at your deaths."

"Very well," she said. "I'm sure you know best. Just as long as Ray can't touch it."

She stood up. "Now, Mr. Crain, I don't want a word of this to leave this office — about Ray, I mean."

"You have my word." Jackson walked her to the door.

"What did she want?" Edna demanded as soon as the door closed.

"A will."

"What else? The old thing wouldn't even look at me when she left. Something's up."

Jackson shook his head. Edna hated secrets.

"I'm going downtown and then home," he said. "See you tomorrow morning."

6

The Broken Oar out on the lake was the preferred hangout for underaged drinkers and adults who liked to take their entertainment away from the prying eyes of the town's solid citizens. It was a long, narrow frame building built on pilings. French doors opened onto a deck outside that reached almost to the water's edge. Inside, a bar extended across one end, and a band platform occupied the long wall opposite the deck. A dance floor surrounded by tables took up the rest of the space. On this, a Tuesday night, Marty Stuart's voice blared from the jukebox in the corner.

Three McBride pushed opened the door and stood for a moment while his eyes became accustomed to the dim interior, then walked toward the back of the room where the back bar was lit with beer signs. BoPeep Jernigan, taking the opportunity while the place was almost empty, was drying and stacking glasses behind the bar. BoPeep was a massive woman of middle age with shoulder-length jet-black hair. Life had dealt her a bad hand, and it showed on her face. But the full tip jar at the end of the bar was a tribute to her ready smile and genuine interest in the triumphs and follies of the patrons of The Broken Oar. And she knew how to keep her mouth shut. For reasons known only to herself, she had taken a liking to Three.

"Hey, young'un," she called as he approached. "Didn't think I'd be seein' you so soon." She put down her towel and drew him a beer in the glass she had been drying. "Sorry to hear about your daddy."

"Yeah. Bummer." Three slid onto a barstool.

"Did you know the cops are looking for you?"

"No shit."

"Well, they're investigatin' your daddy's murder. Where've you been, anyway?"

He swallowed half his beer. "Been staying out at Stinky's cabin. I'll go in tomorrow, I guess."

"Didn't you go to Rockport? I heard y'all had gone down there to fish."

"Weren't biting. We came on back the next day. You don't have to tell that around, though." He raised the glass to his lips and set it down empty.

"Three, you know I don't talk. Refill?"

He shoved his glass toward her.

"You feeling bad about your dad?"

"Yeah. I guess. He was my dad. Know what I'm saying?"

She pulled another beer and pushed it toward Three. "Just because somebody's your parent, that don't mean you've gotta love them — or them you. You want to talk about it?"

Three was surprised to find that he did want to. And BoPeep was the safest person he knew to talk to. "I don't know how to talk about it, Peep. Ask me something."

"Okay. Let me think." She lit a Marlboro and extended the pack to him. He shook his head. "I know. Tell me something about when you were a little kid."

"Hmm. Well, it was pretty good before my mom died, I guess. We used to do all that family stuff together. But Mom would make me mind and he'd back her up. They didn't take no shit, no shit at all." He smiled. "Mom was something else, full of it, if you know what I mean. After she died, he changed."

"How do you mean? Was he mean to you?"

"Oh, hell no. He was all over me, see, wanting to buy me stuff, and take me places. It was like he was trying to make up for Mama's death, or something. My friends were all jealous because every time a new video game or action figure would come out, I'd have the first one in the store. Yeah, that was cool — at first."

"So, what was the problem? Sounds like he loved you a lot."

"There wasn't a problem, not until old Marlene came along, her and her snot-nosed kid."

Just then, two couples came up to the bar and ordered beers. BoPeep filled their order. "Y'all want to run a tab?"

"Yeah," one of the men said. "We'll be over here at a table. Keep 'm coming, will you?"

"You got it." BoPeep smiled at them and turned back to Three.

"So, what happened? Did he stop being good to you?"

"Not that exactly. I just didn't like them around. I was just a kid, you know, and I didn't like when they'd go in their room and shut the door. And they gave the kid the room where I had my video games and my aquarium. I pitched a fit about that, and he made her move into the little store-room off the kitchen."

"Why?"

"Because I didn't like it. Are you paying at-tention here?" He drained his beer and shoved the glass toward her. "See, he was afraid I'd be jealous of the kid. It got to where he wouldn't even look at her. It was funny.

She used to go up and rub against his leg, you know, wanting attention, and he'd just push her away and ask me something like how was school going. Shit like that. I figured out pretty quick, he was trying to suck up to me." He grinned. "Well, I was just a kid, but boy, did I play that for all it was worth. The loot started pouring in. That was when he bought me that big trampoline that took up most of the backyard."

"Well, so did you ever get to liking the wife?"

Three laughed and took a Marlboro from the pack on the bar. He lit it and coughed. "How do you smoke these things? Like her? Not like her, exactly. But after I got to be about thirteen, I learned how to have fun with her."

"How so?"

"Well, see, she's got a temper."

"Strong woman?"

"Oh, hell no. You wouldn't say she was strong, just loud. See, I do something bad, like talk back to her — or just flat-out disobey something she'd told me to do. She'd go tattling to Dad when he got home, and he'd take my part like he always did. Then she'd get mad and start in hollering. Boy, could that woman holler. Then, when she saw she wasn't going to get her way, she'd start crying, and you couldn't shut her up. They'd be in their bedroom, and I'd be out in the hall listening. He'd try sweet-talking her, then he'd get frustrated and go on down to the Wagon Wheel until she cooled down. I learned I could pull off one of those scenes anytime I wanted to. Once I bet my best friend I could do it when he was spending the night, and we both sat out in the hall and watched the show."

BoPeep shook her head. "Didn't you ever feel sorry for her?"

Three looked puzzled. "Why?"

After a moment, BoPeep said, "You poor kid. No wonder you're having such a hard time finding yourself."

"Finding myself? What's that supposed to mean? Shit, woman. I've got it made in the shade. I found myself a long time ago." He pulled some bills out of his pocket and threw them on the bar. "It's all them other folks that can't find me." He laughed and turned away.

BoPeep changed the subject. "Hey, that lady barber your daddy hired has been out here a few times."

"Yeah?"

"She's always by herself. Drinks a beer or two and leaves."

"So?"

"I was just thinking, why don't you ask her out sometimes?"

"Yeah, I might." He strolled toward the door.

"Three," BoPeep called after him. "You get into town and let them know where you are."

Not looking back, Three raised one arm, giving her a backward wave.

Jackson usually felt a sense of well-being when he drove home at the end of a workday. The tree-lined street, Victorian homes and well-manicured lawns of his neighbors represented stability and an abiding connection to the past that, although he had never put it into words, nourished his soul. Patty called him a stick-in-the-mud and teased him because he had never shown an interest in traveling far from home.

"Tiffany's dad was in the Gulf War; Sonny Smart's dad was killed riding in a rodeo. Heck, Daddy, even Ashley's dad, her real dad, went off and worked on an oil rig. Where's your spirit of adventure?"

"I get plenty of adventure right here."

Jackson thought about that conversation as he pulled into his driveway. Maybe Patty was right. Maybe he was a dull guy living a humdrum life. But it damn sure didn't feel that way. He ran into human drama every time he donned his black robe and mounted the bench. And what with two people he was close to being murdered in the course of only two years, well, dull it wasn't. He thought back to last year when his sister-in-law had been brutally murdered. When it began to look as if her husband might be indicted, Jackson, who believed he was innocent, had felt constrained to step in and help solve the case. Now Joe Junior McBride was dead, and although he wasn't family, Jackson's friendship with both Joe and Marlene stretched back to childhood. And it looked bad for Marlene. An axiom in law enforcement holds that the family members of victims are always the first suspects. Jackson knew the sheriff was going to be taking a long, hard look at Marlene, and knowing her as he did, he was certain she was innocent. Unfortunately, he knew too that, as much as he might want to, he couldn't shield her from the ordeal of being a suspect. Too bad Three had an alibi. That boy had exhibited antisocial tendencies from an early age, always in and out of trouble. He was ten times more likely to commit murder than Marlene.

Jackson opened the big front door and

stepped into the cool hallway that always smelled like furniture polish and old wood. He could hear the television blaring from the den. Patty and Ashley must be home. He went into the kitchen and poured two fingers of Scotch into a glass, topping it with ice cubes and took a sip. He had a job to do, and he was poorly equipped for it. He was going to need a drink.

Just before five, Edna had walked into his office and taken a seat in one of the red leather client's chairs in front of his desk. She got right down to business.

"I heard Marlene's kid is staying over at your house."

"That's right."

"Have you talked to her?"

Jackson raised an eyebrow. "What do you think I am? Of course I've talked to her. I said 'Good morning' at breakfast and 'Good-bye' when I left for work. In between I asked how school was going. It's going fine. Thanks for asking."

"Don't get cute with me, Jackson. You men haven't got the sense God promised a goose. Have you talked about the murder? Don't you know that kid's probably all mixed up about everything?" She pulled a crumpled cigarette pack from her pocket and lit up.

Jackson didn't like the way this conversation was going. "I told her about it that night. What else can I do? I figure she and Patty can talk. You know, teenagers, they don't much like talking to adults."

"Jackson, you're just like every other man on the planet. You just plain don't want to because it's uncomfortable." She fixed him with her eyes. "Listen, the kid's just had a murder in her family, and her mama's all doped up on account of she's so *delicate* she can't handle hardly anything that comes along. . . ."

"Come on, Edna, that's not fair. Marlene's had enough to get anybody down."

Edna put her cigarette in the ashtray on Jackson's desk so she could shake her finger at him. "Get real, Jackson. That woman loses it when her hair color don't come out right. Now, somebody's got to be there for Ashley, and you're elected. You get yourself home and get that kid to talk and ask questions. You hear me?"

"Yes, ma'am. But I've got one question. She's got an uncle who happens to be her band director. Why can't he do the job?"

"Hellfire, Jackson. You know how Gerry felt about his brother — *and* about his wife. He's probably more broke up than she is if the truth was known. But he'll carry on because he's got a job to do and all them band kids are depending on him." She rose. "Now get on out of here and do right!"

Jackson took his drink into the den. Patty and Ashley were sprawled on the leather sofas that faced each other opposite the TV.

Patty raised one finger and said, "Hey, Dad," never taking her eyes from the set.

Ashley, on the other hand, rolled off the couch and came to greet him. "Hi, Daddy J." She hugged him around the waist.

Ashley had given him that name when the girls were still in kindergarten. She had adopted him as her daddy with the certainty of a five-year-old that saying it makes it so. And Jackson, flattered, had done nothing to dissuade her, although he often wondered why she hadn't given that affection to Joe Junior. He picked up the remote off the coffee table and switched off the TV.

"Hey!" Patty raised herself up on one elbow and looked at him. "We were watching *T.R.L.*"

Jackson had a job to do, and he was by God going to do it. "We need to talk about what happened over at Ashley's house."

"Oh, good grief, Daddy, we've already

91

had that conversation. It's history."

Jackson looked at Ashley, who seemed fascinated by the portrait of his grandmother that hung over the fireplace. "Ashley? Do you think it's history?"

A tear rolled down her cheek, but she didn't take her eyes off the portrait. "How's my mother?"

"She's fine, just fine . . . no she's not, Ashley. The doctor's given her something to make her rest. It's the best thing for her right now."

"I need to be there with her."

"You do not," Patty shot back. "You need to be right here with us. Now just shut up, okay?"

Ashley ignored this and fixed Jackson with her round turquoise eyes. "Who's there with her? Is Three there? Because if he is . . ."

"No. Three's not there."

"Well, where is he?"

"Gone fishing in Rockport. They haven't been able to get in touch with him."

"Oh, Daddy, he's right here in town. We saw him drive by in his truck on our way home from school."

Jackson stayed on point. He would call and report this to the sheriff later. "Ashley, do you have any more questions?"

"Who's with my mother?"

"Mae Applewaite and some of the other ladies from the church are staying there in shifts. She'll be fine, honey." He patted her on the shoulder. "Have I ever lied to you?"

"Can I at least call her?"

Jackson thought a minute. "I guess that would be okay. Want us to leave the room?" But Ashley already had her cell phone out and was punching in numbers.

Patty and Jackson waited quietly as she spoke, first to Mae Applewaite and then to her mother. When she hung up, she took a deep breath. "She says I should stay here at least for tonight."

"Good." Jackson was glad that was over. "How about we order pizza for supper?"

Ashley, apparently recovered, tossed her red curls and grinned impishly. "Oh, yeah, pizza. Patty would just love it if we order pizza — especially if *he* brings it."

"Uh-oh. He, who?"

"Sonny Smart," Ashley giggled. "Patty's in looove with Sonny Smart."

Patty blushed. "You have to tell everything you know?"

Ashley gripped her sides and giggled some more.

Jackson stood up. "Okay, you girls order. I'm going to read my paper. Call me when it comes."

7

As he left the den, Jackson retrieved the newspaper from the hall table. He went into his study and sank gratefully into his leather club chair. He lit a Don Diego and opened the paper but almost immediately lowered it to his lap. He was having a hard time concentrating on the news of the day. Mandy d'Alejandro's face kept getting in the way. He missed Mandy more than he wanted to admit even to himself. He missed the easy intimacy that had come almost from the day they met, as if they had known each other forever. He had lost himself in the scent of her, her gentle touch, and the soft musical sound of her voice. He had thought it would stay that way forever, that she was the one he would spend the rest of his life with. But one act of his had broken that, maybe forever, and he didn't understand why and sure as hell didn't know what to do about it. Was it a cultural thing? Was his Scottish heritage too logical and analytical to blend with her emotional Latin temperament? Jackson didn't know. All he knew was he wanted her more than he had ever wanted anything in his life, and he was going to figure out some way to get her back.

He picked up the paper and tried to read again, but before he read the headlines, the doorbell rang and he heard the rapid-fire speech of the young, punctuated by high-pitched laughter. The pizza must have come. When Jackson went to investigate, he found Sonny Smart standing at the door with a red-and-blue pizza deliveryman's cap on his head. His face was almost as red as the shirt he wore and Jackson understood why. As he stepped into the hall he overheard Ashley say, "Sonny, aren't you going to ask Patty to the foam party?"

Jackson came to the rescue. "Hey, Sonny. How's your mom? Still working at the Piggly Wiggly?"

"Yes, sir." Sonny removed his cap, and his red hair was plastered down where the rim had been.

"Hat head!" the girls both screamed at once as they ran into the den laughing at their own laser wit.

Jackson took the pizza, paid Sonny and added on a lavish tip for his humiliation. When he went into the den, the girls were rolling on the floor, still laughing uproariously.

"I'm taking this out to the sun porch," he said. "You girls get your drinks and come on out — that is, if you can stop cackling long enough."

"Oh, Daddy . . ." Patty stood up and headed for the kitchen. "You want Cola or orange?" she called over her shoulder to Ashley.

Jackson was relieved to see that Ashley seemed to have forgotten the tragedy at home, at least for the time being. The test would be when the lights went out and the house grew quiet. He hoped that she would be able to sleep without thinking too much.

The girls had ordered pepperoni with mushrooms for Jackson and a large supreme, cut the anchovies, for themselves.

"Good," Jackson remarked, taking a large bite from the steaming triangle in his hand.

"Yeah," Patty said. She turned to Ashley. "Do you know who's taking Stacy Kohl to the foam party? Denton Richardson. Can you believe that? I wouldn't be caught dead with him if you paid me a million dollars."

"I think he's kind of cute in a weird way," Ashley said around a mouthful of pizza. "Anyway, you've got no room to talk, you like Sonny Smart."

Both girls collapsed in another sea of giggles.

Jackson put down his glass. "What is a foam party? You're not going to any party that serves beer."

That brought on a new wave of hilarity. Finally, when she could speak, Patty said, "Oh, Daddy, you don't know anything. A foam party's not beer; it's a party where they fill the whole room up with suds, all the way up to your shoulders, and they play music and everybody dances in it and has a ball. It's a *band* party. Mr. McBride would have a cow if anybody brought beer there."

"When is it?" Jackson asked. "And where?"

"A week from Saturday. It's out at the Whites' cabin on the lake. They've got a boathouse with a concrete floor. Mrs. White is a band mom, and she said we could use it."

Jackson reached for another slice of pizza. "How do they get all that foam?"

Ashley spoke up. "There's a man over in Tyler. He's got a foam machine that he puts something in . . . soap, I guess . . . and it squirts the suds out into the room. Ooh, I can't wait. It is going to be *so* awesome!"

"We get to wear swimsuits or shorts and T-shirts," Patty said. "I'm wearing shorts. What are you wearing?"

"Shorts, for sure," Ashley said. "I won't put on a swimsuit unless I'm going right in the water. I'm too fat."

"You are not. Get over it." Patty pretended to pinch Ashley on the arm.

"Well." Jackson got up and started removing the remnants of the pizza. "I guess if Gerald McBride's letting you do it, it'll be okay."

The girls helped clear the table and went up to Patty's room to listen to some new CDs Ashley had brought with her.

Jackson went into the den and picked up the phone to call the sheriff. Norma Jean, who often acted as dispatcher, answered.

"Norma Jean, this is Jackson Crain."

"Oh, hey, Judge. Leonard's not here. I can get him on the radio, though."

"Where is he?"

"He said he was going to patrol the downtown area because that's Dooley's job and Dooley's off tonight. Tell the truth, though, I expect he's down at the Wagon Wheel having his coffee. That's where he mostly is about this time whether Dooley's off or not."

Jackson chuckled. "I'll just catch him

down there then. If he does call in, tell him I need to talk to him."

"Will do, Judge. G'night."

Jackson decided to walk the short distance to the Wagon Wheel, which sat in the middle of the block on Main Street. A few minutes later he pushed open the glass door and squinted at the bright fluorescent lights. The sheriff was seated on one of the green plastic stools at the counter. Horace Kinkaid sat beside him talking earnestly, most likely angling for details of the murder. Jackson slid onto a stool on the other side of Leonard Gibbs. He ordered coffee from Muriel, the redheaded waitress.

"Sheriff, have you heard anything about Three being back in town?"

The sheriff nodded. "Seems like most everybody in town's seen him. I heard he was staying out at Stinky Brinker's cabin. I can't find him, though. Brinker claims he hasn't seen him, the lyin' little bastard."

"Don't you have an old warrant you could bring old Stinky in on?" Horace asked. "You could bring him in and grill him, threaten to send him to Huntsville if he don't talk."

The sheriff gave Horace a pitying look. "This ain't TV, Horace."

"I saw Three this very morning," Muriel put in. "He came in about six, had breakfast and had me make him some sandwiches for lunch. Said he was going fishing on the lake."

"He can't stay hid forever," the sheriff said. "I'll get him."

Horace had lost interest in the conversation and was looking around the room. "Y'all ought to paint this place. Them walls used to be green a long time ago. Now you can't tell what color they're supposed to be."

"Talk to Rip." Muriel poured more coffee all around. She took the pot and poured more for a customer sitting in a booth along the far wall.

"Hey, who's that?" Horace asked as she came back behind the counter.

"Don't know," Muriel answered. "He's been in here every night for the last three nights."

Sheriff Gibbs and Jackson turned to get a look.

"He looks kinda like old Joe Junior, don't he?" the sheriff said.

"Blamed if he don't," Horace said. "Would you look at that, Jackson?"

The stranger sat hunched over the table, his long, slender hands clasping his coffee mug. He was obviously tall, even sitting down. His hair, cut short, was ashy blond; his nose was prominent but not overly so. Sensing he was being observed, he glanced their way and smiled slightly, as though he knew he was the object of speculation.

"I'm gonna go over there and talk to him," Horace said.

"Hell, Horace," Jackson said, "you're curious as a roomful of cats. Leave the guy alone."

"Yeah, okay. He's probably just visiting somebody around here. Thing is, the more I look at him, the more he looks like Joe Junior. You reckon he's some out-of-town kinfolks we don't know about?"

"Who?" Jackson wondered. "I don't remember Joe mentioning any relatives that lived anywhere but here."

Just then, the sheriff's pager beeped. He took it out of the leather holder on his belt and checked the message. "Gotta go," he said.

"What is it, Sheriff?" Horace asked. "Anything the press needs to know about?"

The sheriff merely grinned and went out the door.

Jackson paid for his coffee and followed.

It was after midnight when Jackson was

awakened by Patty standing over his bed and shaking him.

"Daddy! Wake up, Daddy!"

He was instantly awake. Her voice was frantic.

"Honey, what is it?" He reached for her and pulled her to him. "Are you okay?"

She collapsed against him, sobbing. He could feel her heart pounding.

"Tell me, baby. Has somebody hurt you? Did you have a dream?"

She pulled away from him and started tugging at his arm. "Get up, Daddy. Hurry up! Ashley's missing."

8

As the Wagon Wheel was the preferred gathering place for the men of Post Oak, the Knitter's Nook, just down the street, was the spot where the women got together to socialize and share information about their fellow citizens. Nothing much went on in town that wasn't known at the Knitter's Nook. The place was run by cousins, Esther and Jane Archer. Recently, they had set up two tables in the back room and had begun serving afternoon tea with homemade cakes and pies. It was a great hit with the ladies. Today, business being slow, Esther, Jane, Annabeth Jones, and Myrtice Rice had decided to treat themselves to a rubber or two of bridge.

"Three no trump," Jane announced firmly, eyeing her cousin across the table. "That means I don't have enough for five diamonds, and don't you dare bid it."

"No talking across the table," Myrtice said in a singsong voice.

"I can't help it. Sometimes she doesn't have the brains of a sparrow. Lay down your hand, Esther."

Esther gathered her cards and started to display them in front of her.

"Wait, I haven't bid yet," said Annabeth.

"Well?" Jane held her cards to her ample bosom.

"Pass," Annabeth said.

Esther looked doubtfully at her cards. "Umm . . ."

"Esther, don't . . . you . . . dare!"

"Pass," Esther said.

Myrtice, seated at Esther's left, passed as well.

While Esther arranged her cards face-up on the table, Myrtice spoke.

"Girls, there's a stranger in town. Have y'all seen him?"

Annabeth looked with surprise at Myrtice. "Well, Myrtice, there's plenty of strangers in town. My Lord, people come and go out of here all the time, what with that power plant out at the lake. What about it?"

"This stranger's different; he looks just exactly like Joe Junior McBride." She played the ace of spades and took the first trick. "He's staying over at the bed-and-breakfast. Mr. Rice saw him over there when he went to Rotary." She still referred to her husband in that manner after forty-eight years of marriage. "And here's the thing." She lowered her voice and leaned in to the others. "He was having lunch with Mandy d'Alejandro."

"Ooh," Esther said. "Won't Jackson Crain just die?"

"I wonder if he knows." Myrtice shoved the next trick toward Jane.

Nobody answered. The women concentrated on the game until Jane pulled in the last trick.

"Game and rubber," she said, reaching for the scorecard. "Shall we play another game?"

The others ignored her.

"They're broken up." Annabeth took up the conversation where it had left off. "Don't you remember? You remember, Myrtice. It had something to do with that little girl that was killed here awhile back. She was a cousin or something . . ."

"Broken up or not, he's still sweet on her," Jane said. "Sue Nell Sheppard's daughter, Brooke, is in Patty's class, and Sue Nell says, Brooke says, Patty says he hasn't gotten over her."

"Well, I declare." Esther was stacking the cards and putting them back in their box. "I always thought Jackson had a thing for Marlene McBride. Back when they were kids, I used to see them together all the time."

"That was a long time ago, Esther," Jane said.

"Still, she's a widow again. And she'd be a lot more suitable for Jackson, if you ask me. I know Mandy's a nice Mexican, but she's still a Mexican — and Marlene comes from such a nice family."

"Esther, shut your mouth," Jane said. "That's just not nice."

"And Joe Junior's not even cold yet. The idea!" Myrtice said.

"Hey," Annabeth said. "Maybe that stranger is somebody from the State Historical Commission, coming to see Mandy about that Main Street thing."

"That makes sense," Jane said. "But not half as good a story."

The others laughed.

"Speaking of stories, what's the story on that new lady barber?" Jane started clearing the table. "Hand me that card box, Esther."

"She's a pretty little thing," Annabeth said. "Somebody's out front, Jane. I heard the bell."

Just then, Mae Applewaite came through the curtain that separated the tearoom from the shop.

"Girls! You'll never believe this! Marlene's daughter, Ashley, has disappeared. They think she might have been kidnapped!"

Jackson never went back to bed after Patty came into his room with the news about Ashley. After questioning his daughter, he had alerted the sheriff. He then got dressed, intending to go to the McBride house on the chance that Ashley had gone home. He didn't want to call and alarm Marlene if she hadn't. By now, Patty was back in her bedroom. As he entered the hall, he saw the light shining under her door. He pushed open the door slightly.

"Are you okay?"

Patty was sitting on her bed with her knees drawn up to her chin. "Not really," she said.

"I was going over to the McBrides', but I can stay here with you . . ."

"Uh-uh. You go see Ashley's mom."

"I've called Lutie Faye to come and stay with you."

"Daddy, I'm not a baby. Just go. I'll see you in the morning."

Jackson came and sat on the edge of the bed. "Not until Lutie Faye gets here. Tell me again exactly what happened."

Patty sighed. "There's nothing to tell. I was asleep. I thought I heard something —

like maybe Ashley's cell phone ringing, but when I looked around, she seemed to be asleep, so I dozed off again. I thought I'd been dreaming. I don't know how much later it was 'cause I went back to sleep, but after a while I heard someone walking around out in the hall — or at least it sounded that way. I got up to look and that's when I saw that she, or somebody, had piled her pillows under the cover to look like she was still in the bed. Then I came to get you." She flopped down on her pillow. "Go on, Daddy. I hear Lutie Faye at the back door."

Jackson went down to tell Lutie Faye what had happened. He knew Patty was in good hands. Lutie Faye came in five days a week to cook and clean for him. She had been part of the family since Patty was born.

By the time he got to the McBride home, it was clear Ashley had not come home. An ambulance stood outside the house. Gerald met him at the door.

"We think Marlene may have had a heart attack." His face was distressed. "She hasn't said a word since we gave her the news, but she looks terrible, Judge. The doctor's admitting her to the hospital."

Jackson nodded. He walked down the

hall and looked into the master bedroom, where he found two emergency technicians moving her still form onto a stretcher. Glimpsing her face, he saw that it was ashen. He backed into the hall and joined Gerald. The two men stood at the door and watched as the ambulance attendants wheeled Marlene out and loaded the stretcher into the waiting van.

"I should go with her." Gerald's voice choked.

"You should go home to bed," Jackson answered. "You look like shit. But first I'm going to pour you a stiff drink."

Jackson went to the liquor cabinet and poured a double shot of brandy into a glass. He handed it to Gerald, who took it gratefully. He sank into a chair and downed half the drink in one swallow, coughing as he did so. Jackson took a seat opposite him.

"Better?"

Gerald took another sip of brandy and nodded. "Would you go down there and see about her?"

"Of course."

"And call me in the morning? I'll be at the band hall. We have a phone in there."

"Will do." He watched as Gerald drained the glass. "Another?"

Gerald shook his head. "Have they found Three?" he asked.

"Not yet. Funny thing, though; Patty and Ashley claim they saw him yesterday, driving around in his truck."

"The little bastard!"

"Tell me about him."

Gerald went to the liquor cabinet and poured an inch of brandy in his glass. "I used to feel sorry for him," he said, still standing with his back to Jackson. He turned and gestured with his glass. "Losing his mother like he did."

"So, what changed your mind?"

"It wasn't any one thing. He was a smart kid — mechanical, you know. He could fix stuff that broke around the house when he was only eight. We thought he'd grow up to be an engineer or something. Funny, huh? He grew up to be a sorry, mean, no-account loser."

"When did he start to change?"

"Around third grade, as I recall."

"Was that about the time Joe married Marlene?" Jackson changed his mind and poured himself a small drink.

"No, it was later. He was only six when they married. He seemed happy when Joe told him he was getting married. We talked about it. I said for Joe to go ahead and

110

marry her. The boy needed a mother." He sipped his drink. "I was wrong. He made Marlene's life hell on earth."

"Didn't Joe ever step in — make him stop?"

"Judge, my brother had a blind spot where that boy was concerned. Marlene used to talk to me about it; I was all she had. And I, well . . . nothing. I guess I'd better get on home." He got to his feet. "You'll call me from the hospital?"

"Sure." Jackson followed him to the door. "By the way, the girls were telling me about a band party. A foam party? Are you going to call it off?"

"Can't. It's their one big party of the year. The kids earned the money themselves to pay for it." He took a key from his pocket and locked the front door. "Anyway, it's not until after the funeral. I'll be fine. I've got lots of parents helping with it."

When Jackson got to his office at nine, Edna met him with a cup of hot coffee.

"Call the sheriff right away. He's called three times already."

Jackson, sitting at his desk, pulled the phone toward him and dialed the number of the jail. "Got anything on Ashley?" he asked as soon as Sheriff Gibbs got on the phone.

"Not yet, Judge. We've got the DPS on it. The Rangers won't come in until she's been missing forty-eight hours. What did you find out from your little girl?"

Jackson related what Patty had told him, including the sighting of Three. "Marlene's in the hospital. They were afraid she'd had a heart attack. Turned out it was an anxiety attack. They'll probably let her out this afternoon. Anything else?"

"Yeah, I've got a lead on the boy. Like to drive out to The Broken Oar with me?"

Jackson walked rapidly out the side door of the courthouse and met the sheriff at the back of the jail.

BoPeep, who was alone behind the bar when Jackson and Leonard walked in, was a loyal friend, but she knew better than to lie to the law. She told them all she knew about Three and his whereabouts.

"He said he was staying out at Stinky Brinker's cabin," she finished. "Y'all want a beer? On the house?"

The two men declined and went straight to Stinky's place.

9

If Three was the luckiest kid in his grade, Stinky Brinker must have been the unluckiest. He was born in the cabin where he still lived. His father, Inky Brinker, when he wasn't too drunk to get himself there, worked at the rendering plant. He would come home bringing with him a fetid cloud of decaying animal flesh, and even after he had washed himself at the pump on the back porch, the putrid odor clung to his hair and nails and saturated the air in the tiny cabin. Except on the coldest winter night, Stinky took his blanket out in the yard and slept under a tree. When it rained, he crawled into the henhouse, preferring the company of chickens to that of his father.

His mother was unaffected by the stench. Born with a deviated septum, she was unaware of any smells. Consequently, she was unsympathetic to Stinky and his little brother T.K.'s problem. She declared that having overnight guests upset the hens and inhibited their ability to lay. Leatha Brinker had been saving her egg money to have an operation to correct her deviated septum. When Stinky was thirteen and T.K. was six, she had the operation. A week later, she walked to the highway and hitched a ride out of town. The boys never heard from her again.

A year later, Inky peered into the barrel of a .12-gauge shotgun to see why it had failed to fire. He blew his brains out. The state placed the two boys in foster care, where they stayed for two months before escaping and returning to the cabin. After airing out the place and burning all the bedding and curtains, they moved in. They lived on what they could shoot or steal until Stinky turned sixteen and could get work. Stinky heard later that the foster mother had collected money for their care for almost a year by hoodwinking the over-worked social workers with one lie after another concerning the boys' whereabouts. He imagined the local CPS officers were too embarrassed to report them missing after so long a time.

The road that led to Stinky's cabin was hardly a road at all, just an opening in the trees, overgrown with brush and weeds. Two ruts, tire-width, were barely visible in the undergrowth. You had to look closely, or you might miss them altogether.

Leonard Gibbs knew exactly where to turn. He kept a close watch on Stinky and T.K., partly out of sympathy for them, partly because he suspected Stinky of running an illegal gambling operation. When the car entered the clearing around the cabin, approaching from the rear, a shot rang out.

"Son of a bitch!" The sheriff activated the car's flashing lights and turned on the siren. Steering cautiously, he drove around the side of the cabin to the front, which faced a swampy finger of the lake.

Sixteen-year-old T.K. sat on the front steps holding a rifle in one hand and an open beer can in the other. Empty cans and bottles lay on the ground and on the narrow front porch. A red cooler stood next to the door. T.K. rose and was starting to go inside when the door opened and Stinky, pulling on a torn pair of jeans, came out and ambled across the porch.

The sheriff killed the engine and got out of the car. Jackson followed.

Stinky walked to the edge of the porch. "Hey, Sheriff." He nodded to Jackson. "Whatcha doing scaring my little brother? He ain't doing nothing but shootin' at them turtles over there." He pointed to a line of turtles sunning themselves on a log at the edge of the water.

Jackson looked at T.K. just as he took a furtive sip from the beer can he held. His hand shook. Why was the kid so nervous? Was it a natural distrust of authority, or did he have something to hide?

Leonard Gibbs wasted no time. "We're looking for Three."

"Hey, I ain't responsible for him. How come you think I'd know where he is?" He stepped down from the porch and stood facing the two men. He looked them both squarely in the eye.

At twenty-three, he had the confidence of a much older man. He was short but muscular, with powerful arms, wide shoulders, and narrow hips. His hair, uncombed, was ashy blond; his chest, arms and legs were covered with fine hairs, bleached almost white from the sun. His full lips were turned up in a sardonic grin and one eyebrow cocked upward.

"Don't play games with me," Sheriff Gibbs shot back. "You and him were supposed to go to the coast to fish. Word is, you never went."

"So? Since when is not going fishing against the law?"

The sheriff walked over and took a seat on the edge of the porch as if he had every intention of staying awhile. "You want to tell me where Three is? Or shall I haul you and the kid here off to jail?"

"You can't do that, Sheriff." Stinky reached for a half-smoked cigar in an ashtray on the porch. He lit it with a kitchen match and blew a plume of stale smoke toward Jackson and Leonard. "I know my rights."

Jackson had to admire his self-assurance. And why wouldn't he be confident? He had had to overcome enormous odds just to survive. And, on top of that, he had raised his little brother with no help from anybody. Still, there was apprehension behind that direct gaze as he parried the sheriff's questions.

The sheriff leaned against the porch rail. "Son, are you aware that Three's daddy's been murdered?"

"Heard something." He reached in the cooler and pulled out a beer. "Join me?"

Ignoring the question, the sheriff pressed on. "If Three don't come in and give a statement and at least look like he cares his daddy's dead, he's going to be suspect number one. You understand that?"

"It don't matter whether I understand it or not, does it? I ain't Three. Why don't you go tell him all that?"

"I think you know where he is, son. Matter of fact, I think he's been staying out here with you."

"Yeah, well . . . think what you want to. Hey, Sheriff, I was taking a nap. Mind if I go on back in and finish up with it?"

The sheriff turned red around the collar. "Goddamn right, I care! First, I'm gonna search this house and then I reckon I'll just take you and your little brother in for questioning."

Stinky leaned against a porch support. "On what charge?" he drawled. "And since when can you search a feller's house without a warrant?"

Jackson stepped forward. "Sheriff, I'll take this one." He turned to face Stinky. "The search warrant is in the car, filled out and signed by me, but if you've got nothing to hide, I suggest you invite the sheriff inside to see for himself. Otherwise, the sheriff might feel like he has to make it a real thorough search."

"And I gotta tell you, sometimes I get carried away, don'tcha know, and make a real mess." The sheriff gave him a hard look. "And, by the way, how old's your little brother there?"

"Old enough." Stinky glared at him.

"Hmm . . . I got him figured to be about

sixteen. You give him much beer to drink?"

The boy eased his beer can down on the table behind him.

Sheriff Gibbs, still looking at Stinky, said, "Too late, boy. You've been sucking on that thing ever since we got here. What's the law say about serving alcohol to a minor, Judge?"

"The law takes a dim view," Jackson said. "Up to a year in the county jail and a two-thousand-dollar fine."

"Go on in." Stinky jerked a thumb toward the door and turned his back on them.

The cabin was surprisingly neat inside. The floor, worn pine planks, was swept clean. It was bare except for a worn linoleum rug that distinguished the kitchen area from the rest of the space. A long table against the window wall held a washbasin and a galvanized bucket. Beside that, a dish rack held three plates and three coffee mugs. On the opposite end of the table stood a camp stove with "Coleman" printed on the side. A black cast-iron skillet and a graniteware coffeepot occupied its two burners. The smell of bacon cooking still hung faintly in the air. A marred and scratched farm table sat in the center of the linoleum rug. It was obviously used for both dining and card playing. Cards and poker chips were scattered across it as if a game had just ended.

The rear of the cabin served as a sleeping space. Two army cots and a set of bunk beds occupied the rear wall. They had been neatly made up, with the blankets tucked in, military-style. A wooden ladder led to a loft that extended over this part of the room. A large stone fireplace dominated one wall at the opposite end, fronted by a worn leather sofa and two bent-willow chairs. An army footlocker served as coffee table. A naked lightbulb hung from a cord in the center of the room.

The simplicity of the place made the search go quickly. The sheriff went up to the loft while Jackson searched downstairs. First, he opened the footlocker. It contained clean and neatly folded clothing: three pairs of jeans, several T-shirts, socks, and underwear. Next, he ran his hands over the beds and checked under the mattresses, where he found a Baggie half-filled with marijuana. He pocketed this and called up to the sheriff.

"Anything up there?"

Sheriff Gibbs's ample rear appeared at the top of the ladder. "Nope." He came down, puffing a little from the effort. "Just junk. Tools, old pictures, paper, that kind of stuff. I say we go have another little talk with Stinky and T.K. What do you think, Judge?"

"Right," Jackson said. "I found this." He showed Leonard the Baggie of marijuana. "I think we might be able to trade this for information."

"You're right about that," the sheriff said.

Jackson headed out the door, with the sheriff close behind.

When they returned to the porch, Stinky, a plug of tobacco in his cheek, sat on the front steps chewing and staring out at the lake. T.K. had picked up a sling blade and was cutting marsh grass at the water's edge. Not looking at them, Stinky said, "Well?"

The sheriff tossed the Baggie at him. "Just this. Me and the judge had a little talk about that. We decided we could just forget we ever saw it."

Stinky turned and looked at him with astonishment. "You ain't!"

"Well, not for nothing, don'tcha know," the sheriff said. "We need for you to tell us everything you know about old Three. Everything. Deal?"

"Got no choice, I guess."

"Right you are, son. No choice a'tall. Now, the judge here's got a few questions. You just answer the best you can."

Jackson seated himself on a hide-bottomed chair and lit a Don Diego. "Tell us about the fishing trip. I understand you didn't go. Why was that?"

"We was going," Stinky said. "I got this friend, Lenny, down at Port Aransas. He's got this boat, see, takes parties out to the Gulf on day trips. On a good day, you can pull in trout and big old reds as long as your arms will hold out. Three was all fired up over the trip. Said he needed a vacation — like his whole fuckin' *life* wasn't a vacation." He spat a brown stream at a toad sunning on a rock.

"And?" Jackson said.

"And so we packed up Three's truck the night before and started out before daylight. By the time we got to Jacksonville, the sun was up. We stopped at this Dairy Queen for coffee. I decided to give Lenny a call to let him know when we'd be getting there. Well, Lenny had his nose all out of joint. Seems like some tanker had hit a jetty up around Surfside and spilled out half its oil. That was several days ago, but now big globs of oil were hitting the beaches all the way from Madagorda to south Padre."

"I read about that in the paper," the sheriff said.

"So, anyway, Lenny said you couldn't walk on the beaches or go in the water without getting the stuff all over you. Lenny said sure as hell, he wasn't taking his boat out in that stuff. A thing like that hurts your fisherman's guides right in their pocketbooks."

"That would have been the day before Three's daddy died," Jackson said. "So, you came on back?"

"Yeah, wasn't any sense in going. Three pitched a fit. He's a guy that's used to getting what he wants. He was cussing outside the Dairy Queen — and kicking his truck. I told him to shut up or I'd knock the shit out of him. He calmed down then, and we came on back."

"So, did he stay out here with you — or did he go on home?"

"Stayed. We fished the lake some. Caught a few bream and cooked them up. Slept some and then went over to The Broken Oar until around midnight."

"Was BoPeep there?" Jackson wondered why she hadn't mentioned that.

"Huh? No. Some other old gal was tending bar."

"Okay. So, did Three come on home with you?"

"He was going to, but him and some girl got together. He went off with her, and I ain't seen him since."

"That's the truth?"

"God's truth, Judge. I wouldn't lie for that little bastard. If you think he killed his old man, I got no alibi for him."

Jackson got to his feet. "Well, if you do hear from him, will you tell him his father's funeral is set for tomorrow afternoon?"

"Sure, Judge — if I hear from him."

10

Marlene sat at her dressing table staring into the mirror. She knew she looked haggard, older than her thirty-four years, and the black dress Mae Applewaite had bought her at Goldfarb's only served to accent her pale skin and the dark circles under her eyes. She picked up a hairbrush and then put it back down. Mae and Jane Archer bustled around the room, gathering up her gloves and purse, making sure she had a little packet of tissues inside, and whispering in stage whispers as if the sound of their normal voices was going to send her over the edge. She could hear every word they said. She wished they would just go home and leave her alone. All she could think of now was her precious daughter.

Now Mae was approaching her, holding a glass of water in one hand and a little white pill in the other. "Honey, doctor says for you to take one of these. It'll help you get through the funeral."

Marlene shook her head. Since she had come home from the hospital, she had refused to take the Valium the doctor had prescribed. She needed all her wits about her. Mae retreated, leaving the glass and pill on the dresser. Marlene picked up the pill with thumb and forefinger and dropped it into the wastebasket. She put her chin in her hands and leaned her elbows on the glass top of the table. She needed to think. Joe was gone; she felt nothing. She had known she would feel this way, even looked forward to the day she and Ashley would be free of him and his evil child. Now, none of that mattered. She had to make a new life for herself and her daughter. If everyone would just leave her alone, she thought, she might be able to close her eyes and picture what that life might be. Why hadn't she married Jackson Crain? He would have made a wonderful stepfather. She longed to have Ashley beside her now.

The women's voices intruded on her thoughts.

"What on God's green earth are we going to do with all that food in the kitchen?" This was Mae's voice. "The fridge is running over already."

"Well, for starters, we throw out everything those people from the Holiness Hall sent over. Those people are just nasty!"

"Jane!" Mae couldn't believe her ears.

"They are! Betty Lou Whitlock's sister-in-law joined up with them after a couple came knocking on her door giving out those pamphlets they have."

"You mean Eloise? She never did have good sense."

"One of the twins. It could have been Heloise. Anyway, it was the boy-crazy one. Betty Lou says she only joined because the man giving out the pamphlets was cute."

"Heloise, then," Mae said, looking at her watch. "What's that got to do with the food?"

"Well, according to Eloise, or Heloise, whichever one it was, the men over there are mean to the women. It's part of their doctrine. The women have to do whatever the men tell them to do, and naturally, that would be all the dirty work. The men sit around and discuss important things, like how to get more members to join."

"Just like men," Mae said.

"And you know how they wear those tacky clothes with the hems dragging their ankles. Well, the men make them dress that way."

"The food, Jane. We've got to get going!"

"I'm getting to that. See, Heloise — or

Eloise — was working in the kitchen when a woman put rat pills in the chili."

"No! On purpose?"

"I'm just telling you what Betty Lou told me. But that's not the worst. All the other women just laughed. She said they do that all the time just to get back at the men. It's not just rat pills; sometimes they'll put in fishing worms, chopped up, you know, or they'll add a spoonful of cat food to the tuna salad." Jane picked up her purse. "Betty Lou said her sister-in-law told her that the word would get around among the women when they'd have a church supper: 'Don't eat the meat loaf' or 'Stay away from the dump cake.' "

"That's awful!" Mae said.

"Well, they had to do something." Jane put her hat on. "Those men were awful. Betty Lou told me that at their meetings, they . . ."

Their voices faded as they left the room heading for the kitchen.

Marlene took a deep breath and closed her eyes. After a few minutes of darkness, her mind cleared a little. She thought about Gerald. He loved her, she knew. What a dear man he was. If only she could love him back . . . That was crazy. She shouldn't be thinking that way. Joe wasn't even buried yet. At that moment, Jane Archer came into the room.

"Come on, honey, the limousine's waiting out front to carry you to the church."

The sanctuary of the Baptist church was filling rapidly. Jackson sat in the back pew next to Sheriff Gibbs and his wife, Norma Jean. Edna Buchannan sat at his left. Patty was with the middle-school band, which had come as a group to pay their respects. Jackson had turned down a request to serve as a pallbearer, preferring to sit in back and observe the crowd.

Most of the downtown businesses had closed for the funeral, as was their custom when a prominent citizen died. And Joe Junior had certainly been that. A Rotarian and a deacon in his church, he had served two terms on the town council and one as president of the Chamber of Commerce. His father, Joe Senior, had been mayor of Post Oak for thirty years. But aside from all that, Joe Junior had simply been loved by everyone in town. Jackson could think of a dozen instances where Joe Junior had secretly helped out people in need. He remembered the time Lutie Faye had come to him with the news that her cousin's husband had run away and left her with four small children to raise, one less than two weeks old. Joe Junior had privately supported the family until the baby was old enough for the mother to go back to work. No wonder the ushers had to set up folding chairs in the aisles to handle the overflow crowd. Joe had been a popular man.

It was a mystery to Jackson how that kind and generous man could be the same person that Marlene had described that day in his office, a man who could reject his wife's lonely little girl. Jackson tried to remember what, if anything, he had overheard Ashley say about her stepfather. He couldn't remember anything. Surely, if she was unhappy, she would have talked to Patty, her best friend. He would have to ask Patty about that tonight.

Now Marlene was coming down the aisle, leaning heavily on Gerald's arm. Mae Applewaite followed, trailed by Jane and Esther Archer. Since Three had failed to appear and Ashley was missing, Mae had decided that the three of them would sit with Marlene and Gerald in the pew reserved for the family.

The organ, which had been playing softly, now swelled in volume as the preacher, Brother Smiley, moved to the pulpit. As hymns were sung, prayers said, and eulogies delivered, Jackson's mind wandered to Ashley, who had been missing for two days already. He knew that with each day that passed, her chances of being found alive grew dimmer. Had she been abducted, or had she gone of her own free will? The answer, he thought, was obvious: she must have been kidnapped. Ashley wasn't the kind of girl to go away without telling anyone. Or was she? If she didn't go willingly, why didn't Patty hear anything? Surely, the child would have struggled or called for help.

And who could have done it? Three? Not likely. That wasn't Three's style. He rarely did anything unless it benefitted him, and Jackson could think of nothing Three would gain by risking jail time to abduct his stepsister. Most likely, it was some pervert looking for a female, any female. If this was the case, would he kill her? Or would he keep her hidden somewhere, to be repeatedly savaged according to his needs? Jackson looked at Patty sitting with her band friends. God, what if he had taken her instead? Cold rage swept through him. He would find this monster — and God help him when he did!

Now the congregation was on its feet for the final hymn. "Softly and tenderly, Jesus is calling, calling for you and for me . . ."

Jackson watched the mourners file from the church. He nodded to Mandy as she passed. Muriel from the Wagon Wheel was accompanied by Rip Clark, uncomfortable in a coat and tie. Close behind came Horace Kinkaid and his wife. A tall man followed the Kinkaids. Jackson recognized him as the stranger from the Wagon Wheel.

Just then, Patty came looking for him. "I'm riding to the cemetery with you, Daddy. Okay?"

"You bet!" Jackson said. "Let's go." He put his arm around her and squeezed her tightly.

"Daddy!" She squirmed away from him. "That is *so* not cool!"

Marlene's house was packed when Jackson, carrying a folder under his arm, pushed open the door without knocking. Everyone who had been at the funeral had stopped by to show support and to enjoy the abundance of food that always accompanied a Post Oak funeral.

Mae and the other ladies had loaded up the dining room table with trays and platters piled high with ham, roast beef, and fried chicken. Casseroles of every description vied for space with bowls of creamed corn, mashed potatoes in a sea of butter, black-eyed peas, collard greens cooked with ham hock, and candied yams. Congealed salads in red, green and yellow shimmered in the sunlight streaming in through the bay window. The buffet groaned under the weight of pies and cakes of every shape and size, a large banana pudding (Myrtice Rice's prize-winning recipe), and enough brownies and cookies to sink a rowboat. The townspeople loaded their paper plates and vied for places to sit. They spoke in hushed voices, befitting to the occasion.

Jane Archer, carrying a pitcher of iced tea, approached Jackson as he entered the living room. "Go fill you up a plate, Jackson. Lord, I don't know what we're going to do with all this food."

Jackson shook his head. He didn't know either.

"Where's Marlene?"

"She's back in her room. The preacher's with her, but knowing Marlene, I reckon she'd rather be talking to you."

Jackson wasn't so sure. He knew what was in the file he had in his hand. He walked down the hall and rapped on the bedroom door.

Brother Smiley opened the door, and seeing Jackson, opened it wide. "Come in, Judge. She's been asking for you."

Marlene sat in a chair by the window. "Oh, Jackson!" She burst into tears.

The preacher was at her side in an instant, bending over her solicitously. "There, there, honey. He's in a better place." He opened the bible he was holding. "As it says in Second Thessalonians . . ."

"Oh, shut up!" Her voice rang out like a slap.

The preacher recoiled, a hurt look on his face. "But, sister, if you'd only . . . you know, Jesus . . . He'll . . ." He looked helplessly at Jackson.

Jackson felt sorry for the man. He put his arm around Brother Smiley's shoulders and turned him toward the door. "Let me talk to her. You go and have yourself something to eat."

The preacher nodded. "Maybe that's best." He raised his voice. "I'll be praying for you, sister."

Marlene looked at Jackson and did not answer.

When the door closed, she said, "What's in that folder?"

"It's Joe's will," Jackson said.

The will had been prepared by Bradley Adler, the attorney who had handled Joe Junior's legal affairs. Bradley had called from the Bahamas where he was vacationing and asked Jackson to collect the will from his secretary and reveal its contents to Marlene.

" 'Fraid she's not going to be happy," he'd said in a voice that hinted he'd had a few rum punches and wasn't overly concerned about problems at home.

"Why did you bring it here?" Marlene asked.

Jackson pulled up the dresser stool and sat facing her. "Honey, I know you don't feel much like dealing with this, but it's customary to read the will as soon after death as possible, usually right after the funeral."

"Why?"

"Well . . ." Jackson didn't have an answer to that. He thought it had something to do with the fact that it was a time when all the beneficiaries would presumably be gathered together. In this case, that obviously didn't apply.

"What do I care about that? Where's my daughter, Jackson?"

"The sheriff has called in the Texas

Rangers — and the FBI's in on it now. They've issued an Amber Alert. She'll be found. Try not to worry."

"That's crazy," she said. "Of course I'm worried. Don't I know that the more time passes, the less likely they are to find her? I'm not stupid, Jackson."

"I never thought you were." He opened the folder. "I'll make this as painless as possible, and then, as soon as you feel like it, we need to talk."

Marlene was looking out the window at a mockingbird in a tree.

"Marlene." Jackson opened the will and looked at it, although he knew its contents by heart. "We're going to have to talk about your future — and soon. Joe's left everything he had to Three."

11

Ashley slept, knees drawn up to her chest and hands balled under her chin, like a kitten. She stretched, rolled over and went back to sleep, burrowing deeper into the snug bed and dreamed she was back in her own bed at home. Sometime later, she woke up, stretched again, and opened her eyes, expecting to see her familiar room and finding only blackness. Then she remembered. Suddenly, a thin groove of light etched the darkness under the door. She had learned that when this happened, she was about to be fed. How long had she slept? She had no idea, and she didn't even think about that anymore. Time meant nothing in this new life of hers.

Soon, the up-light in the corner came on and painted shadow patterns on the wall. The straight-backed chair was a ladder, its height magnified in silhouette; the table became a four-legged monster looming over her. And the floor lamp, with its old-fashioned shade, looked like a tall palm tree standing all alone. The lamp didn't work. She had tried it and discovered that the bulb was missing. The only other piece of furniture in the room was the potty chair, the kind they used in sickrooms. It looked exactly like a picture she had seen of "Old Sparky," the electric chair Texas had once used to execute prisoners.

She fell back on the bed and pretended to be asleep. She waited and, sure enough, a figure entered the room, opened the door only enough to squeeze through, set a tray on the table and quietly left. If only she could think, she might be able to escape, but all she ever seemed to want to do was sleep.

After the door closed, she got up and went to the table. She had ten minutes to wolf down the soup and bread and drink the glass of milk with the single oatmeal cookie before the room would go dark again.

She wished the person would say something to her. She was so very lonely.

12

After leaving Marlene's house, Jackson returned to the courthouse, intending to get started on the probate of Joe's will. Thank God, Joe had named him as executor instead of Three. Otherwise, the probate would have to be delayed until Three decided to show himself.

When he pulled his car into his reserved parking space outside the ornate old Victorian courthouse, he felt a sudden reluctance to go inside. Edna would be full of questions and earthy comments. In the mood he was in now, he was liable to bark at her, and Edna, for all her tough talk, was sensitive. He decided to take a short walk before going inside.

He walked briskly away from the building, ignoring the indignant face that glared at him from the window of Edna's office. He turned down Main Street, planning to walk the few blocks that comprised the business district, down one side of the street and then back up the other. He passed the Western Auto and Goldfarb's

Department Store, crossed the street at the traffic light and passed Minton's Drug, where he and Mandy had had their first date. He had impulsively asked her to go there for ice cream the very first time they met. At the end of the block, he crossed over and headed back, past the Wagon Wheel and the Knitter's Nook. As he approached the barbershop with its black wreath on the door, he noticed a light inside. Curious, he stopped and peered in through the glass door.

Gini was inside, sitting at Joe's old rolltop desk. Her hands covered her face; her shoulders shook. He rapped on the glass to get her attention. She looked up, startled, but when she saw it was Jackson, she quickly came and unlocked the door.

"We're not open, Judge Crain."

"I know." He stepped past her and into the shop.

She stood there, uncertain for a moment, and then, self-consciously, her hands went to her hair. "I must look a mess," she said. "I came in to close out the books for the month — I always did that for Joe. He hated that stuff. And then I just . . . I don't know . . . lost it." The words tumbled from her mouth.

"Come and sit down." Jackson guided

her back to the desk. He pulled up a chair and sat facing her.

"I don't know what to do, Judge." She dabbed at her mascara-smeared eyes with a tissue. "Should I try to keep the shop open? Or should I just pick up and leave? Would you ask Mrs. McBride what she wants me to do?"

"Mrs. McBride is in no shape to make decisions right now," he said. "But I have the authority to ask you to stay on — at least temporarily. After all" — he smiled — "the men of this town need you."

"Well . . ."

"Can you handle it?"

"I guess so." Tears welled up in her eyes again. "He was a good man, wasn't he?"

Jackson nodded.

"Do they, uh, do they know who did it . . . killed him, I mean?"

"Not yet, but we'll find out." He put his hands on his knees and leaned forward. "Now, is there anything I can do to help?"

"Not now." She squared her shoulders. "I know what to do."

"Good." Jackson got up and crossed to the door. He paused. "By the way, Gini, the neighbors have seen you driving past Joe's house at night. Is there anything you want to tell me about that?"

"Me? I never . . ." She met his eyes. "Oh, well, I . . . sometimes I go out to that Broken Oar place on the lake. That's probably . . ."

"Good enough." Jackson went out the door, wondering why her knuckles were so white as she gripped the arms of Joe's old swivel chair.

On Saturday, Mandy woke up and stretched in bed. The sun streamed through the lace curtains framing the window, and she remembered what day it was. She had a whole day to do exactly as she pleased, even roll over and go back to sleep. She smiled and stretched again.

"Meow!"

Mandy felt a soft jarring of the bed and instantly a furry face appeared before her, yellow eyes staring intently. She withdrew a hand from the cover and caressed the head.

"Okay, *gatita*," she said. "Outside, it is."

She slipped her feet into the slippers that waited beside her bed and headed for the back door, flipping on the coffeepot as she went.

The calico cat, who was named Patches, followed close at her heels. Mandy opened the screen door and held it. Patches stood, half in and half out, tail high like a flag.

"In or out!" Mandy commanded.

Patches held her ground.

Still wearing her nightgown, Mandy slipped past the cat and onto the deck. Throwing her arms over her head, she stretched yet again and took a deep breath of the fresh morning air. Patches shot past her and eagerly began her morning rounds of patrolling the yard for signs of nocturnal intruders.

This is a perfect day, Mandy thought. The sun, rising over the spire of the Presbyterian Church, would soon dry the dew off the grass and chase away the early-morning chill. It was going to be one of those rare March days where a person could enjoy a tantalizing taste of things to come before the weather relapsed and went back to day after day of rain and fog. Already, bright yellow jonquils bobbed their heads along fences around town, and the two flowering crab apples in Annabeth Jones's yard were bursting with blooms ranging in color from palest pink to deep magenta. In the woods, the dogwoods made their entrance, creating splashes of white against the gray branches of still-dormant trees.

Mandy went back inside, leaving Patches

to her chores and, after first pouring herself a cup of coffee, retreated to her bedroom to dress. Twenty minutes later, she emerged dressed in a pair of pale green slacks and a white cotton blouse. She wore a matching green sweater tied loosely around her shoulders. Her hair, still damp from the shower, was piled loosely on top of her head.

The phone rang. She checked the caller ID first. Mandy refused to answer unnamed calls if she didn't recognize the number. She saw who it was and quickly answered.

"Come over for coffee," Vanessa Largent said without preamble. "The kids are busy with chores, and I have some free time."

Van had been one of the first and best friends Mandy had made when she came to Post Oak. "On my way," she said.

Fifteen minutes later, she was seated at the big farm table in the kitchen of the Rice mansion with Van and Myrtice Rice.

"Where are your men?" Mandy referred to Brother Steve and Ray Rice.

"Gone to cut some broken limbs from the trees in the churchyard." Vanessa sipped her coffee. "The ice storm, you know. They're going to saw them into firewood for next winter."

Mandy nodded. All over town, trees had been damaged from the weight of the ice layer that had covered them.

"I don't imagine Ray's going to be much help," Myrtice observed.

"Now, Myrtice," Van said. "He can help move the smaller branches."

"You know what I mean, Van," Myrtice said. She turned to Mandy. "It's that he's gotten so, I don't know, vague or something lately. I just hope he doesn't wander off."

"Poor you," Mandy said. "How long has this been going on?"

"Not long," Van answered for her. "We're going to ask Dr. Pendergrass if it could be his ulcer medicine."

"Maybe," Myrtice said. "I haven't decided about that yet."

Mandy changed the subject. "How is Marlene? Have you seen her?"

Vanessa got up and refilled their coffee cups. "Saw her last night," she said. "She's definitely not herself — but who would be? I know I'd be a lot worse if it were Steve." She shuddered. "Let's talk about something pleasant. When are you going to let poor Jackson off the hook?"

"Why, what do you mean?" Mandy smiled wickedly.

"You know what I mean. The poor guy's nuts over you."

"Matter of fact, I had lunch with him just the other day. He asked me to go to the fish fry with him."

Van smiled. "Oh, goody. And you said yes, of course."

"I said I'd let him know."

"Jackson's a good man," Myrtice put in. "You could do worse."

Mandy blushed.

"But are you going?" Van pushed.

"I'm going." She ducked her head to hide a smile.

Just then, the swinging doors to the dining room opened and two black boys came in, the twins, Billy and Bobby. Their hands and the fronts of their shirts were covered with soot. They crossed and stood in front of Vanessa.

"Mom," Bobby said, "we're done with the fireplaces."

"Can we ride our bikes to the ballpark?" Billy asked.

"You're sure you got all the ashes? And vacuumed the carpet?"

"Yes'm." The boys both nodded vigorously.

"Then wash up and change and you can go."

The boys grinned widely and ran from the room.

Van smiled after them. "The kids all have Saturday chores," she explained. "It's the only way we can function around here."

"And it's good for them, besides," Myrtice added. "That reminds me, I'd better run upstairs and see how the girls are doing with the bedrooms."

After Myrtice's footsteps faded away, Mandy spoke in a low voice. "How is Mr. Rice, really?"

Van frowned. "I'm not sure. It's not anything I can put my finger on. He loses things, but I do, too. Who wouldn't in a house this size that's spilling over with kids. And he sometimes forgets what you've told him, but he's almost ninety years old. I mean, come on!" She shook her head. "It's not those things that worry me so much . . ."

"What is it, then?"

"It's his eyes. There's something in those eyes, sometimes like . . . like there's nobody home. You know?"

"So, you're going to talk to Dr. P about this?"

"Well, not yet."

"Why not?"

"It's Myrtice, she's afraid people will talk. You know how private she's always been. And I've got to admit, Dr. P can be a bit of a blabbermouth."

Driving home, Mandy thought about the Rices, remembering that only two years ago, the old couple had lived alone in this big house, harboring a tragic secret. It was interesting, she thought, how everybody in town had thought one thing about them, and the reality had been something entirely different. How many other people might be doing the same thing, existing behind a facade of lies. At least one person was dwelling in the shadows and hiding a dark secret, she thought. And that person was the murderer of Joe Junior McBride.

13

Lutie Faye Ivory hummed as she patted a layer of brown sugar over the top of the ham she had just taken from the oven. It smelled good. She hoped the judge and Patty hadn't stuffed themselves with funeral food so they wouldn't have any appetite for supper. When she had covered the meat with a generous layer of sugar, she quickly rinsed her hands under the sink faucet and went to the pantry to get a jar of the spiced peaches she had put up last summer. She expertly rapped the jar, facedown, on the countertop before opening it and emptying its contents into a green mixing bowl.

She was making a special dinner tonight because Judge Crain had confided to her at breakfast that he had a tough job to do today. And he'd told her what it was. He had to give the widow McBride some bad news. The judge often confided in her; he knew she would never say a word to anybody. Wild horses couldn't drag it out of her, if the judge told her not to tell. She sliced the peaches in half and lined them, facedown, on top of the brown sugar. The judge had told her about that barber leaving everything he had to that no-account son of his.

"You mean her and Ashley don't get nothin'?"

"Oh, sure. This is a community-property state."

"Huh?"

"Means half's hers anyway."

"Oh. That don't sound so bad then."

"It's just complicated, is all."

Lutie Faye placed maraschino cherries between the peach halves and sprinkled more brown sugar over the whole thing. She shoved the roaster back into the oven for the glaze to melt.

Butter beans simmered on the stove, smelling of bacon and garlic, and a large salad was ready and waiting in the refrigerator. Now all she had to do was steam the cabbage and slice the pie. She picked up the head of cabbage that was waiting on the cutting board and began shredding it.

Lutie Faye always made a special supper for the Crains on Wednesday nights. On other days, she just came in and fixed breakfast, lunch, and a simple dinner and took care of the house. Of course, that was full-time. Patty had turned into a regular slob since she got to be a teenager. And the judge meant well, but he wasn't so good about picking up after himself, either. He hadn't been that way when Miss Gretchen was alive; she wouldn't let him be. Well, any man will go to seed if he don't have a woman keeping after him all the time.

"Lutie Faye!" The door banged. "What smells so good?" Patty bounded into the room and peeped into the oven. "Ham. Awesome!"

"Where's you' daddy?"

"Getting something out of the car. He'll be in in a minute. Eeyew, gross. Cabbage. I hate cabbage. What's for dessert?"

Lutie pointed to the pie cooling on the drainboard.

"What kind? Chocolate, I hope . . . but coconut's good, too . . . or lemon. It's not caramel, is it?" She flung herself into a chair, straddling the seat and looking at Lutie Faye over the back. "I'll give you a big old kiss if you tell me it's not caramel."

"It's banana cream, and I can do without any kisses. Go comb your hair. We eatin' in the dining room tonight."

Patty made a thumbs-up gesture and untangled herself from the chair. She passed Jackson as he came into the kitchen.

"Umm, something smells good. Do I

have time for a drink before dinner?"

"Take it, if you want it. But, I was fixing to open a bottle of that wine you like so much to go with your ham."

"That sounds good. Can I help?"

"Get the salad outta the fridge and set it in there on the table while I take up these butter beans. How's Miss Marlene doing?"

"Not good." Jackson took out the bowl of greens and retrieved the salad tongs from a drawer in the adjoining butler's pantry.

"You ain't heard anything from Ashley?"

"Not a thing."

"Uh-huh. The longer she stay gone, the more likely it is somebody done hurt her. Poor baby." She sniffed. "Well, go on and call Patty down. We fixin' to eat."

"I'm here." Patty stood at the door. The happy expression she had had when she left was replaced by one of gloom.

Lutie Faye, at Jackson's insistence, always ate with the family on Wednesday nights. Jackson sat at the end of the table with Patty and Lutie Faye on either side of him. No one spoke as they passed around the food and served their own plates.

Finally, Patty said, "Daddy, is it true — that the longer they go without finding Ashley, the more likely she is to be hurt, or . . ."

"Now, don't start worrying yet. She's only been gone a few days. Look at that little girl from Utah. She was gone for months and they still found her." Jackson wished he could take his own advice. He was very worried.

"And look at all those others that turn up dead! I'm not a baby, Daddy."

"I know, honey. We're all concerned. I just mean . . ."

"Your daddy means don't borrow trouble, it'll find you all by itself," Lutie Faye said. "Now, eat your beans. You didn't fill up on that funeral food, did you?"

"I didn't go over to the house," Patty said. "Daddy did."

Lutie Faye looked sharply at Jackson, who shook his head. "I didn't eat a thing."

"I just wish they'd find her."

Jackson changed the subject. "What's the latest on the famous foam party? Is it still a go?"

"Yeah." Patty brightened a little. "Sonny Smart's asked me to go with him. Do you think I should, Daddy? Or should I just go with the girls?"

It was at times like this that Jackson missed Gretchen the most. "I don't know, honey. What's everybody else doing?"

"Most of them don't have dates. Of course that's because nobody asked them." She looked smug.

"Pride goeth before a fall," Lutie Faye quoted. "You just go with the girls. You'll have more fun."

"Oh, Daddy." Patty speared a peach off the platter. "I almost forgot. Mr. McBride asked me to ask if you would be a chaperone at the party."

"Well . . . what do you want me to say?"

"I don't mind. You'd be better than a lot of parents I know. Some of my friends even think you're cool. I don't see why, though."

"Thanks."

"Well, will you do it?"

"Sure, I guess so. How's Gerald doing?"

"Awful, Daddy. He looks awful, so sad. And he forgets what he's told us and what he hasn't. Then he loses his temper."

"Well, I hope you kids will cut him a little slack."

"We do. But I'm worried about him. We've got a marching contest coming up next month, and he needs to get the band in shape for that."

"I'll stop by and see him tomorrow," Jackson said, putting down his fork. "By the way, can I bring a date to the party?"

"Mandy? Sure, everybody likes her.

Anybody else ready for pie?"

The band hall, a red brick building, sat well away from the other buildings on the middle-school campus. A covered sidewalk connected it to the main building. It consisted of a large room for full band rehearsals and several small practice rooms divided by a center hallway. One of these rooms was set aside for Miss Mary Ann Milligan, who used it to teach private piano lessons.

As Jackson approached, cutting across the grass from the parking lot, he heard a riot of sound pouring from the open windows: instruments being tuned, someone practicing scales on a clarinet, and in the piano room the strains of "Für Elise" contributed to the overall din. Outside on the lawn, four majorettes, their faces grim, stood leaning on their batons while Cyndi McMinn, the drum major, barked orders in a shrill voice.

Jackson nodded to the girls and entered by the front door. He found Gerald McBride sitting at his desk, staring out the window at the empty practice field. Jackson tapped twice on the open door and walked in.

"Jackson!" Gerald jumped to his feet and

extended a hand across the desk. "Is there any news?"

"Sorry, no. The officers are doing everything they can. I just dropped in to see how you're getting along."

"Not good."

Jackson could believe that. The man looked awful. Gerald was a stocky man, short but well-built. His usually ruddy face was pale and strained. His head was large for his body, and his reddish hair, which he usually wore in a close crew cut, needed cutting, making his head resemble a large pumpkin. His eyes were round and protruded from their sockets, giving him a perpetually startled expression. Today they were surrounded by dark circles. His mouth was so small that no one could understand how he made so much noise when he was calling out orders to the band on the practice field. He could be heard all the way into the next block. A few of the neighbors had even called the school to complain about the noise. They didn't mind the band's music so much, they said, but the sound of Gerald's voice was driving them crazy.

Gerald leaned across the desk toward Jackson. "Marlene tells me that my brother left everything he had to Three. That can't be right. She must have misunderstood."

"Sorry," Jackson said, "but I can't discuss your sister-in-law's business with you."

"Jackson, I'm family."

"I understand," Jackson said. "Tell you what, the will is going to be filed for probate tomorrow. After that, it'll be public record. Why don't you go down to the courthouse and look at it then? What I'm here for is to talk about that foam party. You sure you don't want to postpone the thing?"

"Can't, Jackson. I told you that. I'll be okay."

"Then I'll be glad to help chaperone." Jackson stood up. "Anything I can do to help you get ready?"

Gerald got to his feet also. "No, thanks. The band moms are handling most of it. Thanks for dropping by, Jackson — and bring a date, if you want to."

Jackson nodded and turned to go. Gerald followed him to the door. "You say the will's going to be filed tomorrow?"

"Yes."

"Fine. I'll go down to the clerk's office and take a look at it. And, Jackson, have they found the little bastard yet?"

"Three, you mean?"

Gerald nodded.

"Not yet. The sheriff will get him eventually. He's been spotted several times around town. For some reason, he wants to play games with law enforcement."

"How stupid is that?"

"Right," Jackson said. "The longer he hides, the guiltier he looks."

"Do you think he killed my brother?"

Jackson shook his head. "Hard to say. We'll know more when we find him."

Gerald leaned against the front of his desk facing Jackson. "Funny thing," he said, "when Three was little, he was the sweetest kid. I always wondered what turned him."

14

"He's flat-out lost his marbles." This was Jane Archer. She spoke in a loud voice to Esther, who was working in the back room of the Knitter's Nook. Jane's arms were submerged to the elbows in a large cardboard box. White packing material flew out the top as she withdrew several objects wrapped in plastic.

"I can't hear you," Esther called from the back.

"You have got to get you a hearing aid," Jane roared.

Esther came to the front, wiping her hands on a kitchen towel. "I can hear just fine. It's you — always hollering at me when I'm working back there. Now, what did you say?"

"Ray Rice."

"And . . ."

"Ray Rice. His marbles, he's losing them. See, I told you you couldn't hear it thunder."

Esther gave up the fight. "Who told you that?"

Just then the bell over the door tinkled and Mae Applewaite came in. "I was getting my prescription filled over at the Rexall when I saw the UPS truck drive off." She leaned across the counter and tried to get a look inside the carton. "Did my number-eighteen needles come in?"

"Don't know yet." Jane continued to extract intriguing packages from the box.

"Okay, I'll wait." She sat down in one of the rocking chairs by the window.

"Mae," Esther said, "do you think Ray Rice is losing his mind?"

"When did he ever have one?" Mae said. "He's been squirrelly ever since I've known him."

"That's the truth," Jane said. "Remember how he used to make Myrtice share a plate lunch with him at the café?"

"And they say he wouldn't let her flush the toilet but twice a day, once in the morning and once at night." Esther giggled at the thought.

"He's been a lot better since Vanessa and Brother Largent moved in there with all those foster kids," Mae said. Mae lived next door to the Rices and made it her business to know what was going on in the large brown mansion on Sycamore Street. "Still, the other morning when I was fixing my coffee, I saw him wandering around outside in nothing but his skivvies. It was cold that morning, too. Remember last Tuesday? Downright nippy for March."

"What was the fool doing?" Jane picked up the now empty carton and set it behind the counter.

"He appeared to be getting ready to rake out the flower bed. He went to the toolshed and got out the rake. I was just about to pick up the phone and call Myrtice when she came flying out the back door and pulled him back inside."

"Poor Myrtice," Esther said.

"Has she said anything to anybody about it?"

"Not that I know of," Mae said. "I expect Vanessa and the preacher must know, though. I mean, living there and all."

Jane had started opening the plastic packages. "You know how she is, proud as a prized rooster. She wouldn't let on she had a problem if it killed her. Here's your knitting needles, Mae. What are you going to make with these big things, anyway?"

"An afghan," Mae said. "You use two strands of yarn —"

"Well, if you ask me, he never was glued too tight." Jane wasn't ready to change the subject. "Oh, here comes Vanessa now.

Don't anybody let on what we've been talking about."

Vanessa Largent came in, a pretty woman with a mane of reddish-blond hair. She wore jeans with a peasant blouse. Her feet, clad in straw sandals, were bare.

"I declare, that Three McBride is going to kill somebody one of these days," she said. "He almost ran over me when I was crossing the street."

"You saw him?" Mae asked.

"Sure. Driving that brand-new truck of his."

"The sheriff's been looking all over the county for him. I declare, that man couldn't find his rear end with a flashlight."

"I saw him day before yesterday at the Sonic," Jane said, "sitting up there at the drive-through, bigger'n Dallas."

"How are Ray and Myrtice?" Esther asked casually.

"Oh, fine and dandy. Miss Jane, do you have any of that baby yarn left — in yellow?"

Jane looked through the yarn bins lined against the wall. "Just two," she said. "Think that'll do you?"

"It should. I'm making a sweater for our new resident, a little Vietnamese baby girl.

She's just the sweetest thing. How much, Miss Jane?"

Jane wrote out a ticket and shoved it across the counter.

"I hope somebody adopts her, soon." Vanessa rummaged through her purse and brought out two bills. "Wait, I've got the correct change." She tossed some coins onto the counter. "She's just too adorable. Well, got to go. Bye."

Mae opened her mouth to say more, but Vanessa was already out on the sidewalk. "Well, so much for that," she said. "That Vanessa, she's always on the run, never time for the least little chat."

"You would be, too, if you had that house to keep and all those kids," Jane said. "Oh, well, we'll find out about Ray Rice sooner or later."

The Wagon Wheel Café occupied a long, narrow storefront building on Main Street. When Rip Clark bought the business in 1970, he tiled the floor in linoleum squares and painted the walls green. He had added a long counter with green-and-chrome stools and a row of green booths along the opposite wall. The center of the room held five separate tables with green Formica tops. The walls were hung with pictures of

Rip and his teammates taken back in the days when he played catcher for the semi-pro Denton County Slammers. As far as Rip was concerned, the decor had stood the test of time, even though the walls were now gray from decades of smoke and grease and the tiled floor, once black and white, was faded and worn away in spots. Several of the barstools had been patched with duct tape. The bench in the rear booth had a six-inch gash in the seat where Jolly Dinkins had cut it with a pocket knife when he was a kid. Now, Jolly was the local undertaker and a deacon down at the Baptist church.

The morning-coffee crowd started showing up at the café every weekday morning at ten o'clock. Today, they were seated around two tables, pushed together in the center of the room. Jackson was present, as were Horace Kinkaid and Jolly Dinkins. Brother Steve Largent was there also. He had once served as pastor at the First Baptist Church before he resigned to help his wife, Vanessa, and the Rices run a foster home. They had converted the old Rice mansion into "Heaven's Haven" and were set up to handle as many as a dozen children on any given day. Vanessa could never turn a child away, though, and from time to time they had had as many as eighteen, occupying cots and sleeping bags all over the place.

The sheriff came in and ordered coffee. Rip filled his order and then poured a cup for himself. He joined the others at the table, leaving Muriel to tend to the counter. This was easy enough, as the coffee drinkers were the only customers in the place. Muriel polished glasses and listened to the men talk.

Horace, who had a nose for news, started the conversation with a question. "Say, Preacher, I hear they're about to cart old Ray off to the funny farm. That right?"

Steve Largent, schooled in the art of deflection, changed the subject. "Have you seen the tulip bed at the park? Over by the fountain? Old Ray did that all by himself. That man is turning into a master gardener."

"Yeah," Jolly said, "he planted daylilies for me down at the funeral home. They're blooming like crazy already, and it's not even April yet."

"We've had an early spring," Jackson put in.

" 'Cept for that ice storm last week." Rip was still sore from his fall.

Horace decided to try another tack.

"Speaking of last week, what's new on old Joe Junior's murder, Sheriff?"

"Could have been an intruder. Jackson, shove that sugar over here."

"You ought to watch your sugar," Jolly said. "I buried your mother not two years ago. Sugar diabetes took her."

"She was ninety-seven," the sheriff growled.

"Sugar ain't the half of it. Did you see how much cream he's poured in that cup?" Rip held up the empty cream pitcher.

"That's not cream," Horace said. "I saw Muriel mixing powdered creamer with water. He just wants you to think you're getting real cream."

"Eat shit!" Rip used his favorite epithet.

Jolly got up and took his cup to Muriel for a refill. "That's even worse," he said, "loaded with cholesterol."

"Speaking of which," Steve Largent said, "is anybody going to the fish fry at the club Saturday night?"

"Guess so," Rip said. "I'm cooking it, ain't I?"

"Larry and I are going," Jolly said, referring to his partner, who, while not a licensed mortician, helped out some with the embalming. "Larry can't decide what to wear."

"Hell, it's a damn fish fry. Tell him to wear a tuxedo," Rip said.

"The wife and I are going," Horace said. "That woman can eat more fish than any two men. God, how she loves the stuff. You going, Jackson?"

Jackson nodded, waiting for the inevitable next question.

"Taking Mandy? Or maybe you're taking the widow McBride. I know you used to be sweeter'n hell on her."

"That was a long time ago," Jackson said. "I'm taking Mandy."

Horace was seated at the end of the table facing the front window. "Well, you better double-check, pal. I just saw her riding by in the car with that stranger — the one that looks just like old Joe Junior!"

15

Jackson tried to call Mandy at her office several times during the afternoon. She never answered. Her office, which was a small converted bungalow just across the street from the courthouse, was visible from his window. He was just curious, he told himself, simply curious, to find out what she had been doing with the stranger. That was all it was, just idle curiosity. Then why did he feel this unease in the pit of his stomach? And this anger? Jackson, who had never been jealous a day in his life, refused to admit that he was now.

When he got home from work that night, Patty was watching television in his study.

"Homework done already?" He kissed her on top of her head.

"Did it at school," she answered, not taking her eyes off the screen.

"What are you watching?"

"It's a video of the band contest at Pine Tree. Mr. McBride said I could bring it home and review it. He said a person could really see their mistakes when they watch these things, and boy, was he right. We look pathetic."

"You won, didn't you?"

"Yeah, well, that's only because Franklin High was having a bad day. What's for supper?"

"Haven't you checked to see what Lutie Faye left?"

"Uh-huh. She's made a pot of that vegetable soup she makes every time she cleans out the refrigerator. You know how that stuff sucks. I thought we could order pizza."

"Sonny Smart wouldn't be working tonight by any chance, would he?"

Patty grinned. "Might be."

"Are you going to let him take you to the foam party?"

"I guess. He said he wouldn't leave me alone until I said yes." She switched off the tape and flung herself down on the arm of the couch. "What could I do?"

"I know. It's hell to be popular."

She threw a throw pillow at him. "Can we order pizza? Please?"

"Sure. Order me a calzone, cheese and pepperoni — and a small salad."

After supper, Jackson picked up the phone and, once again, dialed Mandy's number. When he hung up the receiver, he went to his easy chair and sank down into it. He lit a Don Diego and picked up the newspaper, a satisfied smile on his face.

Three different kinds of potato salad stood on the long wooden tables set up in a grove of trees on the golf course: Mae Applewaite had brought her mustardy brand with red pimento strips for a garnish in a cut-glass bowl that had belonged to her grandmother. Vanessa Largent's tiny new potatoes with the skins left on, with mayo, cucumber and celery seed, was contained in a wooden bowl shaped like a palm leaf, while Jane Archer had put her warm German-style recipe with bacon bits and a vinegary dressing in a green pottery mixing bowl. These delicacies shared space with trays of Caddo Lake green tomato relish, thick-sliced white and purple onions and steaming bowls of corn on the cob floating in a sea of butter. Deviled eggs, olives, pickled okra and homemade peach pickles occupied the space in between the larger dishes. Over to the side, four freezers of homemade strawberry ice cream were being cranked by employees of the club.

As Jackson and Mandy strolled across the golf course to join the crowd already assembled, the scent of frying fish wafted out to greet them.

Jackson took Mandy's hand. "Bet I can eat more fish than you can."

Mandy laughed. "No contest. You've been in training all your life — but don't ever challenge me to a *menudo* eating contest."

"Don't worry." Jackson thought about the spicy Mexican stew made from the stomach of a cow. He gave her hand a squeeze, smiling down at her.

Jackson felt happy, even light-hearted for the first time since Joe Junior's murder and Ashley's disappearance. Tonight, all he wanted to think about was the way Mandy smiled and leaned in toward him when they talked. The tension that had grown up between them in the past year seemed to have melted away, to be replaced by that same easy rapport they had had in the beginning. He was determined, this time, to keep it that way.

As they reached the shade of the trees, they saw that the men were gathered around Rip, who was tossing breaded catfish filets into a large steel pot filled with bubbling oil. The women had gathered in lawn chairs well away from the fire. They sipped drinks and chatted among themselves.

"Looks like this is where we part

company." Mandy extricated her hand from his.

"Not on your life." He put his hand on her waist and guided her firmly toward a secluded bench under a spreading live oak tree. "I'm not sharing you with anybody tonight."

They sat in silence for a few minutes, watching the crowd.

Rip cursed and sweated as he fried the fish. Muriel molded hush puppies and lined them up on a cookie sheet to be added to the oil last. Her new husband, Ron Hughes, hovered nearby, trying to help but mostly just getting in the way.

Jolly Dinkins and his partner, Larry, sat with Vanessa and Steve Largent. Even though it was only March, Larry had on white slacks with a red T-shirt and a navy-blue blazer. He wore loafers on his bare feet.

Mae Applewaite, Annabeth Jones, and Myrtice Rice, dressed for spring, sipped tea in lawn chairs as far away from Rip and his mouth as they could get without appearing to be rude. Ray Rice, looking like a stick figure in a pale blue jumpsuit, stood in the center of the group, talking loudly and waving his arms around.

"Look at Mr. Rice," Mandy said. "He's usually so reserved."

Jackson nodded, remembering the old Ray Rice, a dignified and aloof old man who always wore a shiny black suit, a worn tie and a frayed white dress shirt. Back then he was known as the stingiest (and richest) man in town. Something happened a year ago that had changed him and the town learned that he was not stingy, nor was he rich, only proud. When Vanessa Largent bought the old Rice mansion and, with her husband, Brother Steve, had invited the Rices to continue living in the home they had occupied all their married life, they had gladly taken her up on it. All in all, it had been a happy year. Both Myrtice and Ray seemed to enjoy the active energy the children brought to their home and had participated in their care. It was only lately that Ray had begun to show signs of dementia.

"He sure is lively," Jackson responded to Mandy's remark.

"Too lively. Is he okay?"

Jackson shook his head. "Not really. They want to have him committed — at least temporarily. He's getting to be more than Myrtice can handle."

"Umm. Where's Patty tonight?"

"Spending the night with a friend. Hey! That means I don't have to go home, either.

Matter of fact, she's going to be away two nights."

Mandy smiled and changed the subject. "Any news about Ashley?"

"No."

Just then, Rip began pounding on the old school bell that hung next to the barbecue pits. The crowd surged toward the picnic tables.

The fish was excellent, hot and crisp on the outside and white and delectable on the inside. Everybody stuffed themselves until they couldn't eat another bite.

"I ate sixteen pieces," Horace Kinkaid bragged.

"Well, I wouldn't tell it," his wife chided. "Somebody might find out what a glutton you really are." She smiled. "I already knew it."

Horace threw his arm around his wife's shoulder and gave her a greasy kiss on the cheek. "You love me, though. Don'tcha?"

"She's a glutton, too," Jolly Dinkins put in, ". . . for punishment."

Jackson, who normally would have taken part in the good-natured banter, had other things on his mind tonight. He leaned toward Mandy. "How about a drink in the club?"

Mandy nodded, and after saying good-bye they walked back across the fairway toward the clubhouse.

Inside, the cocktail lounge was deserted except for two men standing at the bar. Jackson and Mandy took a table by a window that overlooked the golf course. The full moon cast a shimmering silver reflection on the pond near the seventh green.

Mandy looked like a million dollars in her Kelly-green sweater and beige wool slacks. The green of the sweater set off her amber skin to perfection, and the lights that danced in the gold hoops in her ears matched the shine in her cocoa-brown eyes. As far as Jackson was concerned, she was perfection in a green sweater. He stared.

Mandy laughed. "Stop staring at me."

"I can't."

"I thought we came in here to have a drink."

"First, I've got to ask you a question — or a favor. You decide."

"Okay."

"Have you heard about the foam party Gerald's throwing for the band kids?"

Mandy shook her head. "What's that?"

"You'll see if I play my cards right. I've agreed to be a chaperone, and I was hoping you'd go as my date. It's next Saturday night."

"Sure, I'll go, Jackson. But I never heard of a foam party. What is it?"

Jackson quickly explained what Patty had told him. "Should be fun to watch." He got to his feet. "Margarita?"

"Coke," she said.

"Sure? Don't you want a screwdriver?"

"Trying to get me drunk?"

Jackson grinned.

He went to the bar and ordered her soda along with a Scotch on the rocks for himself. He slid onto a barstool to wait for the drinks.

"Howdy, Judge."

Jackson turned and saw fellow lawyer, Jason Koti, seated down the bar. Koti, owner of the local title company, specialized in real estate law.

"Howdy, yourself." Jackson swiveled his stool around to face the other man. It was then that he noticed Koti's companion. It was the stranger who looked like Joe Junior's double.

Jackson extended his hand. "Jackson Crain."

"Oh, I know who you are," the tall man said.

Jason spoke quickly. "Jackson, meet Brian Anthony. He's a land man from over in Dallas."

"I'm working out of Jason's office,"

Anthony said, "buying some leases for AmCom Oil."

Jackson nodded. He knew it was common practice for "lease hounds," as they were called, to set themselves up temporarily in a town while they examined land titles to establish ownership and then contacted the owners to purchase mineral rights. They often paid a fee to the title company for the use of their records.

"Going to be here long?" Jackson had seen the man glance over at Mandy.

"About another week if everything goes right," Anthony said, looking once again toward the table where Mandy sat looking out the window.

"Well, good luck." Jackson picked up their drinks and returned to the table.

"I see you met Brian Anthony," she said as he set her drink down.

"How do you know him?" Jackson jumped on the opportunity to ask.

"Met him at Rotary. Jason brought him as his guest last week." Mandy had joined the popular service club soon after moving to Post Oak. She hoped it would help her to spread the word about the Main Street Project, which was not only her job but something she fervently believed in.

Jackson couldn't resist. "That why you

were riding in the car with him?"

Her eyes flashed. "Any reason I shouldn't?"

"Nope." Jackson changed the subject. "How's Main Street progressing?"

Mandy had been transferred from Austin to Post Oak in far northeast Texas to head up the local Main Street Project. Sponsored by the State Historical Commission, the program was designed to revitalize small towns across the state as well as preserve their historical and ethnic authenticity.

Mandy loved to talk about her work. "Going great! We've broken ground on the new park down by the river. It's really going to be beautiful, Jackson. You should see some of the giant cypresses the men found when they started clearing the underbrush. They're breathtaking. And, Jackson, you should see how clear the water . . ."

Jackson loved the sound of her softly accented voice. He relaxed and prompted her to talk more about the various projects she was involved in. He was going to steer clear of the subject of Brian Anthony for the time being.

"I love you," he said, interrupting her.

"What?"

"I said, I love you." He picked up her hand and brought it to his lips.

16

Before dawn Monday morning, Jackson let himself out the back door of Mandy's cottage on Pine Street, closing it quietly behind him. He whistled softly under his breath as he got into his car and headed home to dress for work. Inside, Mandy smiled in her sleep.

He parked in the carport behind his house and went in the back door, closing it softly behind him. He stopped on the back porch to listen for sounds from the kitchen. Sometimes, Lutie came early to start breakfast. Thankfully, this didn't seem to be one of those mornings. He pushed open the door and entered the small sitting room just off the kitchen. He hurried up the back stairs to the master suite, and stripping off clothes as he went, stepped into the shower. It would have felt so good just to stand there, feeling the warm spray pounding his body, and relive the night before. But that was a luxury he couldn't afford. Ray Rice's commitment hearing was at nine and he wanted to meet with the family before the trial. The formal hearing was designed by law to protect elderly and ill people from being sent away for frivolous reasons or for the convenience of others, but it was invariably stressful, and Jackson liked to prepare families for what was about to happen in the courtroom. The law would compel him to put Ray Rice on the stand.

He washed quickly and stepped out of the shower to dress. When he came downstairs, Lutie Fay had miraculously appeared in the kitchen and a breakfast of ham, eggs, grits and biscuits sat waiting on the table.

"Girl, you're a wonder," he said, pulling up a chair and seating himself.

"You are, too." She poured coffee. "I never saw anybody what could sleep all night in a bed and never make a wrinkle in it."

He laughed. So, she had been here all along.

"You want some juice?"

"No, just coffee."

"Where's Patty?"

"Sleeping over at a friend's house. She won't be home until lunchtime."

"She's not the only one that's slept over."

Jackson let that pass. He knew how

much Lutie hated secrets, but this time she'd just have to get over it.

When he arrived at the courthouse, the Rices and the Largents were already seated in chairs outside the courtroom. Ray was dressed in a freshly ironed jumpsuit. His hair, still damp from the shower, was neatly combed. Jason Koti was talking to the family. He would be acting as attorney for Ray. Although, in this case, it was a mere formality, the law required that, like a minor, an impaired person must have legal representation in court.

Jackson walked over to the group.

"If you'll follow me, we'll have a short meeting in chambers before we begin." Jackson led them to a small room behind the courtroom that held only a conference table surrounded by oak chairs. "Please, have seats, all of you."

Jackson seated himself at the head of the table and crossed his arms in front of him. "I know this is difficult for all of you," he said. "Jason and I are going to try our best to make it as painless as possible. That's why I asked you here."

The Largents and Myrtice nodded. Ray bit his fingernail.

"I wonder if any of you have any questions."

"I do," Myrtice said. "Is this going to take long?" Her voice quivered.

"No longer than it has to," Jackson said. "We'll ask you a few questions, the doctor will testify, and then we'll see what Mr. Rice has to say."

Myrtice took a lace-edged handkerchief from her purse and dabbed her eyes. "Judge, I really don't want to do this . . ."

"Then you don't have to," Vanessa said quickly. "We can manage, we can, Myrtice."

"No, we can't." Myrtice's voice grew stronger. "You know what happened last night, Vanessa. Tell the judge about that."

Vanessa sighed. "Oh, Jackson, we lost him again. He disappeared right after supper. It was almost dark before anybody missed him. We searched the whole house and grounds."

"The children combed the whole neighborhood," Myrtice said. "They talked to the neighbors, but nobody seemed to know where he was."

"We were about to call the sheriff," Steve Largent said, "when he came home on his own."

"His clothes were all dirty," Myrtice put in. "And his cheek . . . well, it looked like he had been lying down in the grass. The imprint was still there on his face."

"Before bedtime, Billy, one of the twins, went to get a candy bar out of the jar. He'd done extra chores and was being rewarded. The jar was empty." Vanessa spoke calmly. "We questioned the kids and two of them said they had seen Ray getting candy out of the jar."

Jackson looked at Ray, who was cleaning his fingernails with a toothpick. He appeared to be unaware of what was being said.

"Isn't he allowed to do that?" Jason Koti asked.

"Oh, sure," Vanessa said. "But, you see, the thing was, I had just filled the jar. There must have been twenty bars in there. The kids who saw him said he was taking five or six bars at a time."

Jackson asked a few more questions and then sent them into the courtroom while he got into his black robe. He entered the walnut-paneled room from behind the bench and took a seat.

After calling the court to order, Sheriff Gibbs, who served as bailiff, called the first witness. "Dr. Pendergrass."

Dr. Pendergrass took the stand. The doctor was an imposing man even in his eighties. He had been an athlete during his school days at the University of Texas, and it showed. His arms were still muscular and his shoulders broad. He walked straight and tall. His hair was thick and iron-gray. It was the same color as the suit he wore with a white shirt and red tie.

The doctor had treated the family for many years, had, in fact, gone to high school with both the Rices. It was apparent from his face that he hated being a part of this. He testified that Ray Rice suffered from senile dementia. He also said that he had treated the man recently for scratches and bruises resulting from a fall, although Ray couldn't remember anything about it.

"It's too much for Myrtice to handle," he finished. "I suggested that they send him to Timberland. It's the best facility in Texas for this type of patient."

Jason Koti briefly questioned the doctor. It was a formality. Everyone knew what the outcome would be.

Jackson glanced at Ray Rice. He was watching a cardinal on a branch outside the window. He seemed uninterested in what was happening around him. Once, he nudged Myrtice and whispered something to her, pointing his finger at the bird.

Myrtice Rice was a small woman. Today, her face was almost as white as her neatly combed white hair. Her eyes, red-rimmed but determined, were as blue and pale as an aquamarine. She did not glance at her husband as she took the stand.

Jackson spoke gently. "Mrs. Rice, this is an informal hearing. It won't take long. Can you answer a few questions for us? Try to speak clearly so Edna here can get everything down. Okay?"

Edna Buchannan always acted as court reporter in Jackson's court.

Myrtice's voice was surprisingly strong. "I know, Jackson. I watch *Court TV* all the time."

Jackson smiled. "Then we'll get started. Why don't you just tell us why you think Mr. Rice should go to the hospital."

"Because he's got so I can't keep up with him anymore." Her voice was indignant. "He doesn't listen to a word I say."

"Can you be more specific?" He shot a glance at Ray, who was still looking out the window, although the bird had flown.

"Well, he runs off, don'tcha know — all the time. The very minute I turn my back, he's gone."

"Um-hmm. When was the last time he did that?"

"This morning. I was getting my clothes on, and one of the kids just happened to see him — over in Marlene McBride's yard. He wasn't wearing anything but his underpants." Her voice rose. "Brother Steve had to leave his breakfast and go drag him back home." She looked at her husband, who beamed back at her. "Marlene doesn't need you bothering her, Ray. My soul, she just lost her husband."

Ray Rice smiled sweetly. He patted the arms of his chair.

"See what I mean? He doesn't even know what I'm saying."

"So," Jackson said, "you believe it would be in his best interest to be committed to a hospital?"

"What have I just been saying? His best interest and all the rest of us."

"Just answer yes or no. It's for the record, Mrs. Rice."

"Yes."

Jackson turned to Jason Koti, who shook his head. He scanned the audience while Myrtice returned to her seat. Mae Applewaite sat behind the family, along with Jane Archer and Annabeth Jones. He was surprised to see Marlene McBride at the back of the room sitting next to Amy Tubbs of the EMS.

The Largents testified next. They each told of incidents where Ray had behaved irrationally.

"Once," Vanessa said, "he threw a bowl of cereal on the floor because he said it had blue milk in it. Of course it wasn't blue; it was just milk. Poor thing, he thought we were trying to poison him."

Finally, Jackson addressed the family again. "Now, I know this may seem harsh to you, but we are going to give Mr. Rice a chance to speak for himself. Sheriff, would you escort him to the stand?"

Ray Rice took the witness chair and sat, smiling benignly at the crowd.

"Now, Mr. Rice," Jackson said, "do you know why we're here?"

"No, I don't." The man looked at Jackson, his eyes wide. "Why?"

"Can you tell us what day this is?"

"Sure. It's spring — or summer. Can't you see those leaves out there?" He pointed to the window. "They're green. That's a sure sign."

"Thank you. Now, where are we right now?"

"In church. See the choir section?" He pointed to the jury box. "I don't know where the preacher is, though. Are you going to deliver the message?"

"Thank you, Mr. Rice. You can go back to your seat now."

"Thank you." He nodded courteously

and went back to his seat.

Jackson spoke to the family again. "I'll enter an order of commitment. Mrs. Rice, when do you plan to take him to Timberland?"

"This afternoon," she said. "They've got his room ready."

Ray Rice got to his feet, his eyes suddenly sharp and focused. "I can't go!"

"Why is that, Mr. Rice? We believe it's best . . ."

Tears began to spill from the man's eyes, and his voice quavered. "I can't go anywhere. I've got a job to do. I won't go!" He suddenly bolted and ran from the room.

Myrtice screamed. "Oh, catch him! Please!"

The sheriff, Jason Koti, and Steve pursued him, their footsteps echoing as they ran down the courthouse halls. Jackson, hampered by his black robes, stayed behind.

Vanessa put an arm around Myrtice and led her back to her chair. "Just wait, honey."

"He'll be so scared," Myrtice said. "Oh, poor old thing."

In ten minutes, the men were back. Steve and Sheriff Gibbs were holding Ray between them. Jason Koti followed close behind. They gently set the still-struggling man in a chair. He was making incoherent sounds and spittle ran down his chin.

The doctor turned to Amy Tubbs and nodded. She approached the front of the room with a hypodermic syringe in her hand.

Ray Rice moaned as the needle went into his arm. "The baby . . . who's going to take care of the baby?"

After the hearing was over, Jackson stood in the hall with the family — wished them luck, hugged Myrtice, shook hands with Steve Largent, and nodded to Ray, who was sitting quietly in a chair, the hypo having done its job.

By the time he got back to his office at eleven o'clock, he found Marlene chatting with Edna in his outer office, looking beautiful and almost her old self. Although the circles were still visible around her eyes, she had just about managed to hide them with makeup. The pink in her cheeks probably came from the drugstore, too, but it was progress. At least she'd made the effort. She turned when Jackson came in.

"Jackson, do you have a minute?"

He'd been waiting all morning for a chance to call Mandy, but it would just have to wait. He nodded and followed her into his private office. She took a seat in one of the red leather client chairs in front of his desk. Jackson perched on the edge of the desk, facing her.

"Jackson, I've made a decision. I wanted you to be the first to know."

"Marlene, don't you think it's a little soon for —"

She held up a hand. "Just hear me out. I'm not thinking about doing anything foolish. You don't have to worry." She smiled almost flirtatiously. "It's just that I've decided not to stay buried in the house any longer."

Jackson relaxed. "Sounds good."

"Oh, Jackson, I'm so happy!" She stood up and extended her arms forward, palms up, like a statue of the Virgin Mary. "I've had a vision, Jackson."

Jackson looked into her lovely face. Was she coming unglued? "Tell me about it," he said.

"Joe and Ashley came to me in a dream — only it wasn't really a dream — it was too real for that. They were there, Jackson, standing at the foot of my bed in a circle of light!"

Looking into her eyes, Jackson saw that she believed everything she was saying.

"They were dressed all in white, and the looks on their faces, Jackson, they were so peaceful, so happy." She sat back down. "And they spoke to me, not with words. It wasn't like that. It was like telepathy, you know, with thoughts."

Jackson nodded.

"And they said they wanted me to be happy."

This was getting weirder by the minute. Jackson glanced around the room, wondering what was coming next. His eye fell on his telephone, and for once he was glad to see the red intercom light blinking. Edna was listening in. "Happy?" he said dumbly.

"Yes, happy. And they were real specific about what they wanted me to do."

"What's that?"

"Ashley wants me to go to the foam party. She says she'll be there, too. Only nobody but me will be able to see her. Oh, Jackson, isn't it wonderful? I have my baby back — and my husband, too."

"Marlene, are you . . . ?"

"Sure? Yes, surer than I've ever been about anything in my life. Will you take me, Jackson? Will you be my date to the foam party?"

17

When Ashley lay very still on her cot and closed her eyes and looked, really looked, at the nothingness in front of her, shapes would appear, prism-like and full of color, dark at first, like an old painting where years of dirt and grime had faded the original bright reds and purples and greens. But if she kept her gaze fixed, the dirty film would gradually dissolve and the colors would start to glow and change shape, amoeba-like, shifting and dividing and combining into patterns of every color she could imagine. Ashley thought that if she ever got out of there, she might become an artist so she could capture this panoply in paint.

She was thinking more now, thinking and even beginning to plan, because she had figured out something. She had learned, quite by accident, that she was being drugged. It had happened two days ago — or was it a week? She had no way of measuring time except to count how often the food came. The milk had been a little off that one day, and not wanting to offend her captor, she had taken the glass and emptied it in the sink in the corner. After finishing the rest of her meal, she had lain back on her cot expecting sleep to come as it had done before. When it didn't she had sat up, and then got to her feet. Her head began to swim, so she sat back down again. After a minute, she tried again, this time rising slowly. She felt a little stronger, so, arms outstretched like a blind person, she began to explore her surroundings.

The room was square, she discovered, with brick walls and a concrete floor. Now she came across a window on one wall, boarded up. She ran her hands around the window frame, crying out once when she scraped her finger on a nail. She felt a crack under the boards. It was small, but wide enough that she could just reach her fingers through it and feel the fresh air outside. She put her eye to the crack, but all she could see were dead leaves and pine needles. This window must be at ground level, which meant her room must be in a cellar or a basement. She extended her fingers out again. It felt good; at least part of her was out.

Since then, she had disposed of her milk the same way, and every day she grew stronger, her mind sharper.

Then, one day, she pulled a candy bar out from the crack under the window. It was fresh, a Hershey bar. She ate it and then put her eye to the spot where the candy bar had come through. She could see a little light filtered through a curtain of green grass.

The next day, she found an oatmeal cookie, wrapped in plastic wrap.

18

Jackson Crain had been one of the reasons Mandy had decided to stay in Post Oak, Jackson Crain and the trees. Unlike the wide, low live oaks, thorny *ouichache,* and weedlike mesquite she had grown up with in south Texas, these east Texas trees spoke up for themselves; they had presence. Pine, sweet gum, sycamore and elm. Their tops seemed to reach for the sun while their roots dug deep into the rich, dark, loamy soil. And when you drove down a country lane, their branches stretched toward you, meeting in the middle to form a watery tunnel of green. In autumn, they splashed the woods with flamboyant flames of ocher, orange and crimson against a backdrop of black-green pine. In spring, they put on a more genteel show of peach-blossom pink, redbud red, and dogwood white and filled the air with earthy perfume.

Unlike Jackson, the trees had never let her down.

She sat at her desk and looked at the phone. She was still reeling from his announcement that he wouldn't be taking her to the foam party after all; he was taking Marlene McBride. Later, she knew she would be very angry; now all she was was numb.

She got up and turned the sign in the window to "Closed." She turned the knob on the door's dead bolt and went back to her living quarters behind the office. She put on the kettle and made herself a cup of tea. Then she sat down at the kitchen table to wait for the anger to rise up in her. It would be far better than the hurt she was feeling now — and the sickening suspicion that she had been used.

Jackson hung up the phone in his office. All in all, things had gone pretty well, he thought. Mandy had accepted the news without saying much. At least, she hadn't reacted angrily. After all, she knew he loved her. Hadn't he told her that at least four or five times at the fish fry? She was a reasonable person. She would understand why he couldn't say no to Marlene while she was in such a fragile state.

He put his chin in his hand and looked out the window, remembering their first meeting. It had been at the grand opening of the Main Street offices, a ribbon-cutting ceremony. The mayor gave a speech, and Jackson had gone only because Patty would be playing with the middle-school band. But when he saw Mandy standing on the steps wearing that yellow dress, he was glad he had come. The two of them had walked away together when the ceremony was over. It was then that they had started talking; they hadn't stopped since. They talked, and then later kissed, at his house and at her house, in the car and in the woods, in restaurants and at the homes of friends. And always, there was always more to learn about each other. They talked about their past loves, their families, and their dreams for the future, which they agreed, but never actually said out loud, would be together. They talked about God and what they liked to eat; they talked about politics and their favorite books, movies, music. In the end, they agreed on the important things. The rest, well, that only made the connection more interesting. They crawled into each other's heads and bodies and both found themselves at home.

Jackson admitted that there had been that one bump in their relationship, a misunderstanding. Mandy had accused him of going behind her back to check up on her when he had visited her home town of Victoria. It wasn't true, of course. He had been working on a murder case. But that was behind them now. He smiled and picked up a file in his in-box. Might as well get some work done. Mandy understood; he was sure of it.

Jackson picked Marlene up at eight. Gerald had told him that the chaperones didn't have to get there all that early because he had already recruited several of the band-booster parents to put out the food and pass out soft drinks to the kids. He drove the car down the narrow lane that led to the Whites' boathouse and parked well away from the dozen or so cars and the yellow school bus that were already there. Marlene wore jeans with a white shirt tied at the waist. She had on turquoise earrings and smiled when he opened the door for her.

"It feels good to be out again," she said.

"You look beautiful, like your old self."

"It was hard, Jackson, real hard. But now that I know they're gone, I have to make myself start living again." She turned and started to walk down the lane toward the lights of the party.

Jackson caught her arm and turned her

toward him. "Marlene, you don't know Ashley's dead."

"She's dead, Jackson. A mother knows. Just don't go there, okay?"

"Okay, babe." He gave her hand a squeeze and led her down the path toward the lights and sounds around the boat-house.

Spotlights mounted on trees illuminated the tables where adults presided over trays of sandwiches and cookies and big bowls of chips and popcorn. They saw Mae Applewaite and Vanessa Largent standing behind the drinks table. A few kids in shorts were milling around outside, but most of them were inside playing in the chin-high foam that filled the room and spilled out every time someone opened the door.

Word had spread about the party, and it looked as if the whole town had turned out to see the show. Groups of adults were sitting in lawn chairs all around the perimeter of the clearing, well away from the action, but close enough to see and hear everything.

Jackson and Marlene strolled over to where Mae and Vanessa were adding more ice to a cooler of drinks. "Let me do that," Jackson said.

"We're finished." Mae flipped down the

cooler's lid. She came around and gave Marlene a hug. "I'm just so glad to see you out, honey."

Marlene smiled. She fingered a stack of towels on the end of the table. "Why all the towels?"

Mae pointed toward the boathouse. "You'll see when one of them comes out," she said. "Y'all want a drink?"

Jackson took a root beer and Marlene had a Diet Pepsi.

"Can we help?" Marlene sipped her drink and looked around.

"Just keep an eye on things," Vanessa said. "Watch for the ones that keep going to their cars. Beer's always a possibility, even at this age."

"Jackson," Mae said, "Vanessa's got a new kid. Had you heard?"

"I saw her out in the yard," Marlene spoke up. Her house was just across the street from the Rice mansion. "Cute little blonde."

"Right." Vanessa sat down on a folding chair. "Kristi, with a *K*. She's fourteen and practically an orphan — just the sweetest little thing. She's been a big help with the little ones."

"Where did she come from?" Jackson wanted to know.

"Tyler. Her daddy killed her mom when she was ten. He's in prison. The poor kid's been passed around ever since." She opened a canned cola and took a sip. "I hope we can keep her."

"Well, let me know if I can help," Jackson said.

Gerald came out of the boathouse and approached them. He was wearing shorts and a yellow T-shirt with "Post Oak Fighting Bulldogs" printed on it. Foam hung off his body, making him look like a sad, melting snowman. He picked up a towel and mopped his face and neck.

"Somebody remember to lock me up if I ever agree to do this again," he said. He walked over and kissed Marlene on the cheek. "Glad to see you out, hon. Mae, can I have a Coke?"

"Is Patty in there?" Jackson asked.

"In the thick of things." He took a drink from the can Mae handed him. "She and Sonny haven't stopped dancing. It's like the inside of a washing machine in there. The more they dance and jump around, the more suds they make." He laughed. "Well, I'd better get back inside."

Jackson looked around for a place to sit. "I should have brought some lawn chairs."

"Gerald brought chairs for the

chaperones," Mae said. "Look over there, against that tree."

Jackson picked up two of the aluminum chairs and set them up on a little rise, where they could see everything. Horace Kinkaid and his wife were nearby.

"I think I'll circulate," Marlene said. "Do you mind?"

"Be good for you," Jackson said.

Horace turned his chair around to face Jackson. "Since when are you squiring the widow McBride around?"

"You planning on writing a feature story?" Jackson grinned at his nosy friend.

"Nope. Just wondering where the little Main Street lady is."

"Home, I guess."

"Come on, buddy, I thought you two were hot and heavy."

"Marlene needed to get out of the house. Mandy understands."

Horace pointed to the path leading from the parked cars. "Yep. She understands all right — maybe more than you think."

Jackson turned and followed Horace's pointing finger. He saw Mandy and Brian Anthony walking slowly down the hill. Brian leaned in close to her and said something, and she laughed, looking up into his eyes. Jackson felt anger rise up in him as he watched. What kind of game was she playing? When they got to the clearing, the couple stood for a moment talking to Vanessa and Mae. They got drinks and went to find seats across the path and away from where Jackson and the Kinkaids were seated.

Glancing at the boathouse, Jackson saw three soapy figures come out the door and head up the hill toward him.

"Daddy!"

He hadn't recognized Patty until she spoke. She walked toward him, arms outstretched and stiff-legged, like the Mummy, soapsuds oozing off of her like rags.

"I am Ozymandias, king of kings," she said. "And these are my royal attendants."

"Hey, hon," Jackson said. "Having fun?"

"It is so awesome," Patty said. "You ought to come in there, Daddy."

"And have you die of shame. No, thanks. Hi, Sonny."

"Hey, Judge."

"Daddy, this is Kristi. She's new."

Jackson nodded gravely at the pigtailed girl. "Pleased to meet you, ma'am."

Kristi giggled.

"You're living with the Largents, I hear."

"Yes, sir."

"Like it here in Post Oak?"

The girl nodded, soapy pigtails bobbing up and down.

"Daddy, we didn't come out here just to make small talk. Something's happened that I thought you ought to know about."

"Yes . . . ?"

Marlene walked up. "Hi, Patty and Sonny," she said. "Who's your friend?"

Patty's face flushed, exasperated. She sighed. "Hi, Mrs. McBride." She quickly made the introduction.

"Now, as you were saying . . ." Jackson addressed Patty.

"Not now," she hissed, glancing at Marlene, who was talking to Sonny. She stood still for a moment, thinking, and then said in a loud voice, "Daddy, I left my backpack in your car, and there's something I've got to get out of it. Go with me, okay?"

Jackson made a move toward his pocket. "Here, I'll just give you the keys."

"*Daddy . . . go . . . with . . . me.*" She spoke through clinched teeth.

"Okay, sure."

Patty was already hurrying up the path. Jackson caught up with her. "What's this about?"

"I don't need anything from the car," she

said. "I just wanted to get you alone. Daddy, Three McBride's here."

"Are you sure?"

"Of course I'm sure, Daddy. I saw him with my own eyes."

"Where?"

"We were dancing. It was a slow dance, and I was dancing with Matthew Davis. You know, boring Matthew Davis? He came up and asked me to dance while Sonny was in the rest room. What could I do? You don't want to just *step on* a person's feelings, you know."

"Moving right along . . ."

"Well, I danced with him, but I sure wasn't going to close my eyes and look like I was having a good time, you know, so I was looking around at all the other dancers. Most of the boys are so short. It's pathetic. The girls' heads just —"

"Could we get on with it?"

"Okay, I happened to look out the window, the one on the back side of the building, and there he was, Three McBride and that old Stinky person he hangs around with. They were looking at us through the window. Spying. How gross is that?"

Jackson took her by the shoulders. "You're absolutely sure?"

"Daddy, I know what I saw. When they saw me watching, they ducked real quick. Mr. Gerald saw him, too."

Jackson already had his cell phone out. "What did he do?"

"Well, the dance got over, so I, kind of casually, you know, went over to the window and peeked out. Mr. Gerald was out there talking to them. I couldn't hear what they said, but before they left, he shook hands with both of them. What's that all about?"

"Don't have a clue." He dialed the sheriff's number and waited for an answer. "Yes, Norma, is the sheriff in? . . . Okay, can you get him on the radio? . . . Fine, have him call me on my cell as soon as you get him."

When he clicked off the phone, he gave Patty a quick hug. "You did the right thing. Now, I want you and your friends to go back to the party. Have a good time, but stay in the boathouse or in the clearing where the adults are. No going into the woods! Understood?"

"Understood." She nodded vigorously.

Just then, Jackson's phone rang. He quickly told the sheriff about Three having been seen. "Okay, Sheriff. You'll keep and eye on things? Thanks." When he clicked off the cell phone, he gave Patty a quick hug.

"Is the sheriff coming?"

"He's sending a car out to patrol the area. They won't come around the party unless it's absolutely necessary."

"Good."

The party broke up at ten. Gerald herded the kids, who had toweled themselves dry, into the school bus. The driver was to take them back to the band hall, where they would be picked up by their parents. Jackson, knowing that Sonny's mom would take Patty home, asked Marlene whether she wanted to stay and help with the cleanup.

"Sure!" She started helping the ladies clear the food away while Jackson went looking for Gerald. He opened the door and found himself in a small entry hall. A French door separated it from the main room which, he could see through the glass, was still shoulder-high in foam. He decided against going inside.

He was standing by the door when Gerald approached him. "Thanks for helping out."

"No problem. What else can I do?" Jackson indicated the boathouse.

"Not much, tonight. We'll have to wait

for this mess to melt. Where's Marlene?"

"Helping the others." He turned to go back to the clearing.

Gerald fell in step with him. "I just want to tell my sister-in-law hello."

Marlene was saying good-bye to some of the band parents when they arrived. "All finished out here," she said. She patted Gerald on the shoulder. "You throw a good party, brother-in-law."

Gerald looked at her with affection. "It's great to see you out again."

Her face clouded. "Life goes on," she said.

"Well, I'd better get back in there and finish up." Gerald turned to go.

"Want help?" Jackson asked.

"No, thanks. Most of it will have to wait until tomorrow." He turned to go back.

"You're sure?"

Gerald was hurrying back down the path. "I'll see you soon." He waved and disappeared into the building.

Jackson nodded and turned to Marlene. "Ready?"

"I guess." Marlene was looking at Gerald's retreating back.

"Anything wrong?"

"Oh, I don't know . . . no, I guess not. Let's go. Oh, wait, I'm getting a call." She pulled a cell phone out of her jeans pocket. "Mae? What?" She listened. "Your wallet? No, I didn't see it. Okay, no problem. Bye." She shrugged and replaced the phone in her pocket.

"I didn't hear that ring," Jackson commented.

"It vibrates. Mae's left her billfold inside. I'll run in and get it for her."

"Want me to go?"

"No, thanks." She was already running down the path to the boathouse. Ten minutes later she returned, shaking her head and apologizing.

"It wasn't where she said it was. Sorry I took so long." She held up the wallet. "It had dropped behind one of the tables."

Back at Marlene's house, Jackson walked her to the door and kissed her lightly on the cheek. "You're a real classy lady," he said.

She paused at the door, looking back at him. "Jackson, was Three there tonight?"

"Why do you ask?"

"I overheard somebody talking. Tell me the truth, Jackson. I need to know."

"Are you afraid of him?"

"I don't know . . . a little, maybe."

Jackson took her arm and guided her to the porch swing. He sat down beside her and took her hand. "He was seen there. The sheriff was notified. He may have him in custody right now."

"Can you find out?"

"Sure. I'll let you know. In the meantime, I want you to make sure you lock all your doors and windows. You'll be fine. Want me to stay for a while?"

She squeezed his hand. "It's tempting, but no. Just call me as soon as you know anything. Okay?"

"Right."

He saw that she was safely in her house and then drove home through the darkened streets. The light was on in Patty's room when he let himself into the house. He went directly up to check on her, kicking himself for not having been home when she got there.

She was sitting cross-legged in the middle of her bed, a laptop open in front of her.

"Have a good time tonight?" he asked.

"It was wild!"

"Good wild, or just wild?"

"The best. We're going to do this every year."

"Have you consulted Gerald about that?"

She grinned. "Nope. But I think he had a really good time, too."

19

Marlene was startled awake by a nightmare, and the agony of the last week came flooding back. She had dreamed she was skidding down an icy mountain road in a big, heavy eighteen-wheeler, desperately clutching the wheel, negotiating the hairpin turns, trying to put off the crash that was sure to come. She sat up in bed, holding her head in her hands. How could she possibly have thought that life was going to be normal again? Joe and Ashley were never coming back. She might as well face facts; her life was over. It was simply cowardice that had made her put off what had to be done. She got out of bed, opened the medicine cabinet and took out the bottle of sleeping pills she had gotten refilled yesterday. Next, she retrieved a second bottle, the one she had been saving.

Sheriff Gibbs sat at the kitchen table in the living quarters of the jail. He was having a second cup of coffee and enjoying the morning paper.

"Paper says they've opened a new computer store on Main Street."

"Hmm . . . ," said his wife, Norma. She came and stood behind him, holding her own mug of coffee. " *'Kuntry Kumputers.'* Doesn't sound very high-tech to me."

"Sure don't. Hal Henderson's boy, Randy, is running it. He graduated from Texas Tech last spring and then couldn't get a job on account of all those companies going broke, so Hal just set him up in business."

"Nice." Norma Jean sat down at the table and buttered a biscuit. "I wonder who thought up the name."

"Hal's wife, probably."

"What kept you out so late last night, hon? I don't even remember hearing you come in."

"Who else? Three McBride again. Some kids saw him hanging around the party. Me and Dooley rode around half the night looking for him, but the little weasel got away again."

"He's just playing games with you. That makes me so mad, I could . . ."

The sheriff smiled at her. "Settle down, old woman, we'll get him. You gotta be patient, is all."

"I guess. Do you think he killed his dad?"

"Could have. So far, he's the best suspect we've got, but that's only because he keeps hiding out. We'll get him, though. Got any more coffee?"

Norma picked up the coffeepot and re-filled his cup. "Sounds to me like he's the only suspect."

"No, you're wrong, hon. The wife's still in the running — and old Gerald. They both had the opportunity." He sipped his coffee. "Um, you make the best coffee in town."

"You drink too much. It's bad for your blood pressure."

Sheriff Gibbs had heard this before. "What have you heard about the new lady barber old Joe hired?"

"Why would I know?"

"Don't give me that, old woman. I know you stay on the phone half the day with your lady friends. They must be saying something."

"Well, as a matter of fact, I heard she was running from the law."

The sheriff laughed. "Who said that?"

"I heard that when I went into the Knitter's Nook to pick up some embroidery thread." She grinned. "But I also heard she was a transsexual and had been a man up until two years ago."

He looked at her. "You're putting me on."

"Yep. And that's what you get for asking me things like that. I don't gossip and you know it."

"Yeah, you're right. Oops, there goes the phone."

He went into his office to answer. When he came back, his face was clouded.

"There's been another murder," he said.

Mandy d'Alejandro stood in the shower washing her hair, a chore she usually enjoyed. She liked the warm mist surrounding her and the clean herbal, woodsy scent of the shampoo she used. This morning, she hardly noticed. She was feeling troubled and a little out of control. She hadn't meant to flaunt her date with Brian in front of Jackson. Anyway, she rationalized, it hadn't really been a date, just two people meeting by accident and deciding to go for a drive together. She had run into Brian at the Conoco, where she had stopped for gas. He had been filling his own tank at the next pump, and after they got to talking, as any civilized person would do, she thought, he had asked her to go have a cup of coffee with him. Then it had seemed the most natural thing in the world for them to take a drive in the country.

She stepped out of the shower and dried herself. Automatically, she reached for the Halston cologne Jackson had given her last Valentine's Day. Oh, great, she thought, now I feel even worse. She quickly towel-dried her hair and began roughly combing out the tangles.

How was she supposed to know Brian would drive straight out to the foam party? And wouldn't she have looked like a fool if she had refused to get out of the car? She was still smarting from the look Jackson gave her when he saw her there.

She stepped into her underwear and snapped on her bra. The thing was, she hadn't even been mad anymore. Once she had cooled down, she realized that it was the right thing for Jackson to do, taking Marlene to the party. Mandy knew he loved her. Now, he thought she had been playing some kind of adolescent game with him. Pulling on her dress, she thought, I'll just have to make it right again — if I can.

She picked up the phone and dialed his office. Edna answered.

"Edna, it's Mandy. Is Jackson there?"

"No he's not, and he's got a shit-load of paperwork piled up on his desk. The sheriff called the minute he came in, and he went running out of here. The Lord only knows when he'll be back."

Jackson followed Sheriff Gibbs into the boathouse. Dooley Burns stood outside waiting for the crime scene investigation team to arrive. In sharp contrast to the shouts and laughter of the night before, the place was eerily silent. The foam had dissipated except for small patches that clung to the soggy shag-carpet remnants Gerald had gotten from the furniture store and laid down to keep the kids from slipping. The scent of wet wool, mildew, and blood hit them like a slap when they entered the room.

"Over here." The sheriff pointed to the still form of Gerald McBride, lying in a fetal position on the floor. A butcher knife protruded from his back.

Jackson followed as the sheriff stepped in the spaces between the carpet scraps. "Probably no usable footprints, but I'm not taking any chances until the crime scene guys get here."

Jackson looked down at Gerald. A large pool of blood had left the body and saturated the carpet under him. "It must have taken him a long time to die," he commented.

"That's what I'm thinking," the sheriff

said. "Looks like he lay here bleeding for quite a while."

Jackson looked at the body, wondering how long he had waited under all that foam before the life finally drained out of him.

"When's the last time you saw him, Judge?"

Jackson let his mind go back to the night of the party. "Saturday night, we were the last to leave," he said. "Marlene and I offered to stay and help, but now that I think of it, he seemed in a hurry to have us go."

"Odd," the sheriff said. "Suppose he was meeting somebody — like maybe his nephew?"

"Possible. Or, he just wanted to finish up and get out of here."

"Then wouldn't he have let y'all help him?"

Jackson shook his head. "Not necessarily. He's always been pretty much of a loner. I guess he just didn't want company. That's probably why he wasn't missed all day Sunday."

The sheriff wasn't giving up. "He could have wanted y'all out of there for some reason we don't know about. Here comes the team. We'd best stay out of their way."

Jackson, the sheriff, and Dooley stood

outside the boathouse while the team went over the building, both inside and out. After more than an hour, Lieutenant Bridger of the crime lab joined them.

"Not much to go on," he said. "We got one good footprint off the carpet. You folks haven't been walking around in there, have you?"

The sheriff looked pained. "I know better'n that, Mike."

Bridger wasn't so sure. "The knife had prints, of course, but they're pretty smudged. Looks like he lay there under that foam for a good hour before he bled to death."

"See if you can get a match with Three McBride," the sheriff said. "You got his prints on file, that's for sure."

"Anyone else you know about?"

The sheriff looked at Jackson.

"Patty said Stinky Brinker was out here, too," Jackson said.

"Okay. Anyone else?"

"A lot of people came to watch."

"Sure. We'll run Three and Stinky. I should have a full report on your desk in a couple of days, Sheriff. We'll need at least a week for the autopsy."

"Gotcha."

An ambulance stood waiting. The sheriff

motioned for the attendants to come and get the body.

The three men stood and watched as the corpse, in a black body bag, was rolled out on a gurney and was loaded into the ambulance.

"Poor guy," Dooley said. "Them band kids are sure gonna miss him."

"Damn!" Jackson had forgotten all about the kids. They would have to be told, and before the news was spread all over town.

"Judge, would you go by the school and let the principal know? I reckon I'll have to tell Mrs. McBride."

"I'll take care of that, too." Jackson had his cell phone out. He dialed Marlene's number and spoke briefly into the phone. "She's out," he said.

He dialed Mae Applewaite's number and asked her to go over to Marlene's house and wait for her to come home. "Call me the minute she gets there."

The sheriff listened.

"Something's happened. No, I can't tell you now . . . Yes . . . As soon as she comes home . . . That's right . . . No, Mae, I can't tell you any more than that . . . No, we haven't found Ashley. Just do this for me, okay? Thanks." He pressed the off button.

"That woman's plumb eat up with the nosy," the sheriff said.

20

Jackson drove directly to the middle school and told the principal what had happened. He knew that the school had procedures in place to deal with situations like this. The teachers and counselors would be notified, and they would tell the students.

Counseling sessions would be arranged class by class, and the students would be encouraged to talk about it. And any students who required it would be offered private sessions. While he was tempted to take Patty out of class and talk to her himself, he was pretty sure she would handle it better if she heard the news along with her classmates.

He drove past Marlene's house, but saw that her car was not in the driveway. Since he was in no mood to field any more questions from Mae, he drove on to his office.

Edna looked up from her computer screen when he walked in. "Where the hell have you been, Jackson? The goddam phone's been ringing off the wall."

"Gerald McBride's been murdered."

"Holy shit! Has anybody told Marlene? That woman's not going to be able to take much more."

Jackson went into his office and sat down at his desk. Edna followed. "Well, have they?"

"She's not home. Mae's over there waiting for her. She's going to call me as soon as Marlene gets in." He sighed, suddenly tired. "Then I'll go on over and tell her."

Edna sat down on one of the red leather client's chairs. "Jackson, that's not your job."

"Somebody's got to tell her."

"Sure, but it doesn't have to be you. Hell, Jackson, Brother Steve Largent lives right across the street. Let him do it; that's his job."

"But —"

"Jackson, since when is your name Jesus H. Christ? Can't you let somebody else take on the hard jobs once in a while?"

"Maybe you're right." He picked up the phone and dialed the minister's number.

While he was talking, Edna went to her desk and came back carrying a stack of pink phone message slips. She slid them across the desk to Jackson. He hung up the phone and began to go through them. He pulled out the one from Mandy. "All this stuff can wait until morning," he said. "That all?"

"Just one other thing. That land man that's working out of Jason Koti's office dropped by."

"Brian Anthony? What the hell did he want?" He glared at her.

"Well, shit, don't kill the messenger. He said he needed to talk to you and that it was important. I made him an appointment. He'll be here at three."

Jackson looked at his watch. Twelve-thirty. Suddenly, he was starved. He remembered that Lutie Faye had taken the day off to go to a cousin's funeral; he had left the house without breakfast.

"Had lunch?" He looked at his secretary.

"Ate a sandwich an hour ago. Go on and eat, then get back here and get some work done."

"Right." He stood up from his desk. "I'm going over to the Wagon Wheel. Call me over there if you hear from Marlene. Anybody else can wait until I get back."

"What if Mandy calls?"

"What?"

"You heard me. Y'all had a falling-out. You know there's no secrets in this town. So, what if she calls?"

"Call me at the café. Nobody else. Got it?"

She gave a thumbs-up sign and went back to her desk.

Jackson picked up the phone and dialed Mandy's number. After four rings, the answering machine picked up. He hung up the phone in disgust.

The Wagon Wheel was crowded. Not only was the usual lunch crowd there, but also packed in was a busload of senior citizens who had come to town to visit the museum and shop in the antique stores up and down Main Street. Every table and booth was taken.

Jackson found a seat at the counter next to Horace Kinkaid, who was polishing off a double bacon cheeseburger. Rip Clark was wiping off the counter and doing the best he could to ignore Horace's running comments.

"Hey, Jackson," Horace said. "I was just tellin' Rip here about how I couldn't hardly find my meat patty in this hamburger." He pointed to his plate.

Jackson nodded, waiting for the punch line.

"Then I looked under the pickle! Right, buddy?" Horace reached across the bar and nudged Rip.

"I thought that joke was funny the first

time I heard it — back in '57." Rip set a glass of water in front of Jackson. "Plate lunches are all gone."

"I'll just take a bowl of stew," Jackson said, "and some corn bread, if you've got any left."

"In that case, you'll be having yesterday's plate lunch," Horace said with a grin.

Rip rolled his eyes. "Ain't you got a ribbon-cutting to cover? Them's all you ever read in that rag of yours — that and the want ads." He dished up the stew from a Crock-Pot behind the counter and set it in front of Jackson, along with a handful of saltines. "Corn bread's gone," he said.

Horace turned to Jackson for help. "Tell him, Jackson. Tell him what a fine newspaper I run over here. Hell, if anything would ever happen in this town, I'd be all over it like ugly on an ape."

Jackson, his mouth full of stew, winked at Rip.

"The barber gettin' murdered ain't news?" Rip said. "Hell, you buried that on page four so you could fill the front page with the Chamber of Commerce banquet."

"Those are my advertisers," Horace explained. "A paper don't pay for itself, you know. Tell him, Jackson."

Jackson wiped his mouth with a paper

napkin. "Gerald McBride was murdered last night."

"What?" Horace pulled a pad and pencil out of his pocket. "Well, why didn't you say something? Where? How?"

"Talk to the sheriff," Jackson said. He finished his stew and pushed some bills across the counter at Rip. "I've got to go."

Back at his office, Jackson stopped at Edna's desk. "Any calls?"

Edna looked up from her computer. "Patty called from school. She was crying. I told her I'd get ahold of you and send you right over there, but she didn't want me to. Said for me to tell you she'd be okay, and for you not to worry. She just wanted to ask you about the band director."

"I'm going over there."

"Jackson, no. You didn't let me finish. After I talked to her, she settled down and quit crying. She told me the counselor was meeting with her class fifth period. She wants to be there for that."

"If she was crying, she needs me. I'm going."

Edna sighed. "Stop being bull-headed, Jackson. After we hung up, I called the school and talked to the principal. Mrs. Smith said she should stay for the meeting. She's going to let Patty's teacher know she was upset. They'll take good care of her. Jackson, let the kid grow up."

She was right, of course. Jackson nodded and went into his office. He intended to tackle the mountain of paperwork on his desk. He worked steadily until three o'clock, when Edna opened his door.

"Brian Anthony's here."

Watching Brian come toward him, Jackson was again struck by how much he resembled Joe Junior. Even the slight slope of his shoulders, as if he were accustomed to having to stoop to get through doorways, was the same. His hair, sandy and not so thin as Joe's, grew in the same straight line across his forehead, and his ears were large and lay flat against his head. His eyes were the same shade of blue but sharp and inquisitive, while Joe's had been calm and amiable. He took a seat in one of the red chairs and placed the briefcase he'd been carrying on his lap.

Jackson folded his hands in front of him and waited.

"Judge, let's get one thing out of the way before we start. I'm a married man. I have no interest in your girlfriend."

Jackson opened his mouth to speak and then snapped it shut and waited for the man to continue.

"I had to find out some things about you before I came here."

"Why?"

"I needed someone to confide in. I thought about telling the sheriff, but I decided you were the man. Frankly, I don't know who to trust around here."

Jackson nodded. "Go on."

"I suppose you, like everybody else I've met, have noticed that I bear a striking resemblance to your deceased barber."

For the first time, Jackson noticed that the man had a slight accent. English? He nodded. "We've noticed."

"I'm three years older than Ian — or Joe, as you called him."

"So, what's your story?" Jackson was getting irritated with the man.

"You . . . well, in for a penny, in for a pound. Our mother used to say that. By that, I mean mine and Joe's mother. We were brothers."

"No way," Jackson said. "Joe lived here all his life. I knew his parents, went to school with him. You can't be his brother. That's crazy." But he knew it wasn't crazy. It was the only explanation for their incredible likeness.

Brian held up his hand. "I'll explain. Our mother brought us here from Australia when I was seven and Joe was four. She was a single mom when that wasn't as common as it is now. Computers were just taking off, the big ones, and she was a smashing good keypunch operator. There weren't too many of those around at that time. We settled in San Francisco. There was a man in it, too, of course. Screwed our lives up royally."

Jackson nodded.

"Mom met him in Melbourne. He'd come over for a conference of some kind. Our mom was a real beauty, the kind men can't resist. Sexy, in an innocent way, if you get my meaning."

Jackson nodded again.

"He promised her a job and a life in the States, if she'd come to San Francisco to live. Poor Mom. She was a fool to believe him, and he ruined her life for her. Married, of course, and only out for a good time. He told her he'd divorce his wife and marry her, but he didn't want to be saddled with kids."

"The son of a bitch!"

"In spades. But, you see, our mom was in deep shit. She had no money and didn't know a soul over here. He told her if she didn't get rid of us, the deal was off. No job; no relationship; no marriage."

"So she put you both up for adoption, and Joe ended up here. End of story. Right?"

"Not quite. Yes, she put us in foster care, and yes, Joe was adopted. Being older, I was harder to place. I remained in foster care."

"Rotten deal for two kids."

"Rotten deal for our mom, too. See, she didn't want to do it. She just didn't see any other way out. You see, all that time she was thinking they'd just take care of us for a while — until she could get us back. She never even knew what she was signing when she signed away her parental rights. Anyway, while we went out to foster homes, Mom went to work for this guy's company — and started keeping company with him. Not that she intended to marry the bastard now. She was just play-acting until she could make enough to get us back and go home to Australia."

Jackson frowned. "Pretty drastic."

"I told you, she couldn't see any other way out. She was young, only twenty-seven. Don't be too hard on our mom. Well, after a few months, Mom found out she had a lot more talent than she thought, and she'd made a few friends over here. She dumped Joe Cool and took a better-paying job. Now, she thought, she could just go back to the state and tell them that things had changed and they'd give us back to her. Well, she was half right. It took her a while to convince the California child protective people that she could be a good parent, but finally, she did. They returned me to her." He paused. "All this talking is making me dry. Don't suppose you've got anything to drink?"

"Soda okay? Or water?"

"Cola would be fine. Diet."

Jackson pressed the intercom button. "Edna, could we have a couple of diet colas?"

Almost immediately, Edna came in with the drinks, eyeing Brian curiously as she set them down. When she left, Jackson noticed that the intercom button still glowed red. He shut it off and heard an angry thud from the next room.

Jackson sipped his drink. "So, you said they gave you back to her. What about Joe Junior?"

"I would have thought you could figure that one out. He'd already been adopted by the McBrides."

"But they lived in Texas."

"Wrong. They lived in Oakland. What happened was they adopted my brother. It was all legal, but at the time our mother decided she could take us back, the adoption hadn't been finalized. There's a waiting period."

"Yes, I know," Jackson said.

"So Mom got a lawyer. It took most of the money she'd saved, but she was determined to get Ian back, and she almost did, too."

"What happened?"

"Well, her lawyer went into court and asked for the adoption to be overturned on the grounds that Mom had been in an impossible situation and she didn't know what she was signing when she signed us away. It was looking good. She and her lawyer showed up for the final hearing; the McBrides had been ordered to bring Ian to the courthouse. They never showed up. You see, they'd taken my brother and run away to Texas with him."

"They could have been extradited."

"Right. But she would have had even more legal fees to get the whole thing straightened out. Her lawyer, the bastard, wouldn't do another thing until she paid him another five thousand. It might as well have been a million. Mom was broke. She thought she'd save up some more money and go back to court, but then she got sick and couldn't work for a year. By the time she'd saved up enough money, another two years had passed. Then it was just too late. She hired a private investigator to look into my brother's situation in Post Oak. He came back and reported that Ian was with a good family and doing well. It just seemed to her that it would be cruel to up-root him again. By this time, you see, she'd started to drink. Our household wasn't all that pleasant."

"I see. So, why are you here — now?"

"Okay. Well, I grew up pretty fast — had to. There wasn't any money for me to go to college. We had moved to Seattle when I was fourteen. Mom still worked in com-puters and was still a whiz at it — when she was sober. Thing was, those times were getting fewer and fewer. I got out of high school and went to the police academy. When I was twenty, Mom died. Now that I was alone in the world, I decided to look up my brother. Long story, short. I found him using my police contacts, and we've been communicating ever since. That's what I really came here to tell you. Sorry it took so long to get there."

"It's okay. So, what have you got?"

"I wanted to tell you that I know who killed him, and I can prove it."

He opened the briefcase and withdrew a stack of papers.

21

After Brian Anthony left, Jackson got up from his desk and stood at the window staring out at Post Oak. As long as he could remember, it had been a peaceful place, a place where nothing much ever happened. Except for the occasional spat, people generally got along with one another. It was like a family, he thought, people were born here and died here, they fought and made up, married and divorced, raised their children and watched them go out into the world on their own. He now knew that this town, his town, would never be quite the same again. For a long time to come, little Post Oak, Texas, population five thousand, would be remembered as the town that spawned a monster.

He focused on the scene outside. The hardware store on the corner had put out its lawnmowers and hammocks and barbecue pits. Annabeth Jones stood on the sidewalk admiring the hanging baskets in front of the flower shop. And across the street, the little yellow bungalow where

Mandy lived and worked had red geraniums growing out of the concrete pots in front. As he watched, Mandy herself, dressed in a blue sundress, came out with a watering can and watered the flowers. His heart lurched.

He went back to his desk, dialed her number again. This time she answered.

"Mandy, it's me. We need to talk."

"I know."

"Can I come over now?"

"Jackson, I don't know. I'm confused right now."

"Brian Anthony was just here."

"So?"

"He said there was nothing going on between you and him. I'm sorry I ever thought any different."

"You could have asked me, Jackson."

"You're right."

"Just give me a little time. Okay?"

After hanging up the phone, Jackson sat with his head in his hands. He was startled when the intercom buzzed loudly.

"Jackson, the school's on the phone. It's Mrs. Jones, and she says it's important."

Everybody's message is important, he thought. Nobody ever thinks what they have to say is a minor matter. He picked up the phone. "Hello, Frances."

"Hi. Jackson, I wonder if you could come over here and get Patty."

"Why? What's wrong?"

"Nothing, really. We're letting some of the students go home early — the ones that have been the most upset by Gerald's death. Patty's fine, really, but since she cried this morning, I just think it would be good if she could spend some time with you. Mrs. Bridges, the counselor, agrees."

"I'm on my way."

Ten minutes later, he pulled up in front of the school. Patty was standing outside with four other students, also waiting for rides.

"I feel like a wuss," she said, getting into the car. "They made me go home. I didn't want to."

"You've had a shock, baby. Anyway, now I get to spend some time with my favorite daughter."

"Drive off quick, Daddy. I think I'm about to cry again."

He put the car in gear and pulled away from the curb. "Where to? Want to go for a milkshake?"

"I just want to go home. Is Lutie there? I want to see her." Her voice cracked.

"She's there. She said she'd come over and cook supper for us after her cousin's funeral."

At home, Jackson parked the car in the carport. They went in through the back door and were greeted by the homey smells of food cooking.

"Umm, meat loaf," Jackson said.

"And chocolate cake." Patty went into the kitchen and hugged Lutie, who was peeling potatoes.

"Be careful before you cut yourself." Lutie held the paring knife over her head. "What's the matter with you? And how come you're home so early?"

"Oh, Lu-Lu." Patty used her baby name for Lutie. "Somebody's killed Mr. McBride."

"Well, don't I know that? That was a spell back."

"No, not that."

"Somebody's murdered Gerald," Jackson said.

"Oh, honey." Lutie stroked Patty's hair. "Come on over here and set down." She led her to the kitchen table. "Lemme cut you a piece of cake."

"I wouldn't mind a piece, too." Jackson tried for a light tone. "And some coffee, if it's made."

Lutie cut two slices of cake. She poured Jackson a cup of coffee and one for herself.

"You want some milk, hon?"

Patty nodded.

They sat silently around the table, the adults searching for the right words to console Patty. Patty nibbled at her cake and sipped milk. She was the first to speak.

"How can everything be so good one day and so bad the next? It's just not fair!" Her face crumpled.

"God never promised you no picnic," Lutie said. "And trouble makes us strong."

Patty put down her fork and looked from Jackson to Lutie. "I don't want to be strong. I want my best friend back, and her daddy back — and Mr. Gerald, too. I just want things to be the way they were." She pushed her half-eaten cake away.

"Honey, why don't you go up and have a nice warm bath and a nap? I'll come up and rub your back, like I used to when you was little," Lutie said.

"Yeah, I might." She pushed her chair back from the table and stood up. "Daddy, will you stay home? I don't want you to go anywhere."

He looked at his watch. "Well, I . . ."

"He'll be here. Now, you run up and get in that tub. I'll be on up directly."

When Patty disappeared up the back stairs, she turned to Jackson. "You ain't got nothin' more important than stayin' here with your girl right now."

"Lutie, something's come up. I've really got to —"

"Now, you listen to me, Judge. This little girl's already lost her mama. Now her best friend and her daddy and her teacher are gone. Don't you know, she's afraid she's gonna lose you, too? Give her the rest of this day. By mornin' she'll most likely be ready to go back to school. Kids bounce back."

22

Ashley had eaten the sandwich that had been left for her and poured the milk down the drain. She was still hungry, so she made her way over to the slit at the bottom of the window and felt with her fingers for a candy bar. There was none. She pressed her eyes against the crack and watched the world at grass level. At night, it came alive. Beetles with eyes that glowed in the dark were captured by toads with long tongues. Occasionally, a snake would come by and swallow up a toad. Cats passed, walking low and silent as they stalked some hapless field mouse, or howling their awful howls when they mated. Once she had seen an owl swoop down and seize a cottontail rabbit.

She wondered sometimes if she would ever get out of this place. And, if she did, would she look like Gollum — all white and hairless, creeping along on all fours?

She went back to her cot and lay down, staring into the blackness above. She said the Lord's Prayer in her mind and then,

"Now I Lay Me Down to Sleep." She was pretty sure there wasn't any God to hear her, but she said what she could remember of the Twenty-third Psalm, just in case.

23

Edna had news when Jackson got to his office the next day. "Mae Applewaite called early. She said to tell you that Marlene got home okay. She'd gone over to Tyler to do a little shopping." She set a mug of coffee in front of him. "She must be getting better, I guess."

Jackson nodded. "Guess so. Anything else?"

"The sheriff called. Wants you to call him as soon as you get in. Hell's bells, Jackson. Can't that man do his job without you? You've got commissioners' court on Monday first thing, and you've got a shit-load of paperwork to get done."

"If I have to, I'll work this weekend. Now, get out of here and let me call Sheriff Gibbs."

She grunted and left the room.

Jackson had had plenty of time to digest the news Brian Anthony had given him. He made up his mind to keep the information to himself for the time being. He lit his first Don Diego of the day and dialed the sheriff's number.

"Judge, I got a right peculiar phone call this morning."

"What was that?"

"BoPeep Jernigan called. You know who I'm talking about?"

"Sure. I know BoPeep. Waitress out at The Broken Oar. Right?"

"Right. Well, she said she had some important information about the case. Said I should come out there at nine o'clock."

Jackson checked his watch. "You'd better get going. It's eight-thirty now."

"I know. I was waitin' for you to get in. Any chance you could go with me? BoPeep said she'd like it if you could come. I get the feeling this might be a breakthrough. Something in the woman's voice."

"Pick me up in front of the courthouse."

The "Closed" sign was up in the window of the old tavern when the two men stepped up on the wooden porch. However, the door opened immediately, and BoPeep held it for them to enter. The place was totally dark except for a small light behind the bar.

"Hey, Sheriff. Hey, Judge. Y'all come on back here to the office."

She led them through a door behind the bar which opened into a tiny office. There was just room for a sofa and a rolltop desk with a swivel chair. Three McBride and Stinky Brinker sat on the shabby sofa, which was pushed against the wall opposite the desk. The sheriff instinctively put his hand on his gun.

"Where the hell have you been hiding out, boy?"

"Ain't no cause for that, Sheriff." Stinky's voice was composed. "Three here's got something to say."

BoPeep went into the bar and came back with two straight chairs for Jackson and Sheriff Gibbs. She lowered herself into the desk chair. "Y'all sit down here and listen to what he has to tell you," she said.

The sheriff held up his hand. "Don't say a word, son, until I read you your rights." He took a card out of his shirt pocket and began to read. "You have the right to remain silent. You have the right to have an —"

"Stop!" Three jumped up and made for the door. "I'm not going to jail!"

Stinky followed and grabbed him by the arm. He guided him back to the sofa and pushed him down. "You ain't goin' nowhere. You're innocent, and the sheriff's a fair man. Now, you tell these fellers what you know — just like you told me and 'Peep, here."

Three glared at him. "They won't believe me. I don't know why I let you talk me into this."

"Talk!" Stinky snapped.

"Tell them, honey," BoPeep said. "I been knowing the sheriff all my life. He's straight as string. Start at the beginning."

"Well . . . okay. But they won't believe it. Who would in this town?"

"Give it a shot," Jackson said. "Who knows?"

"Okay. Uh . . . well, I guess I'd better start at the first. That would be when I was four or five — right after my mom died. I missed her like crazy. I was young, but I remember it like it was yesterday. Dad was so cut up about it that, for a while, he forgot all about me. When I did anything to get his attention, he'd look at me like he'd never seen me in his life. I was one lonesome kid — stayed in my room most of the time." He looked out the window at the row of pine trees that grew around the lake. "Don't think I'm trying for sympathy here. I'm just telling you. Okay? See that old dead tree out there? That's the way my dad was, just hollow inside, like part of him had rotted away."

"Poor little kid," BoPeep murmured.

Three glanced at her and went on. "One

day, I noticed a difference in my dad. Not much at first, just that once in a while he'd look at me like he saw me. You know? Like he was finally really seeing me. And he'd ask me how my day had gone, and stuff. Things got a little better every day. Once in a while, he'd even smile at me."

The sheriff shifted in his seat and glanced at his watch. Three noticed.

"Look, I know you don't have all day. I'm making this as short as I can, but you've gotta understand how everything got so screwed up."

"Take your time," Jackson said.

"Okay. So, anyway, one day he came home early and asked me if I wanted to go for ice cream. Naturally, I was tickled to death and went racing to the car." He scowled. "Marlene was sitting there, and her kid was strapped in a car seat in back."

"Uh-huh." The sheriff had pulled out a small tablet and was taking notes. "I guess you didn't like that much."

"That's where you're wrong. You don't know me, Sheriff. You just think you do."

"Go on," Jackson said.

"Dad introduced them to me. She was real sweet and pretty. Marlene, I mean. I liked her right off — and the kid, Ashley, was okay. Well, pretty soon the two of them were around most of the time. Marlene was nice to me. I was beginning to forget Mama, not really forget her, I don't guess, but now I had a woman around to hug and kiss me and, you know, bake cookies and stuff."

"So, what turned it around? How did you end up enemies?" Jackson said.

Three looked at him sharply. "I wonder how you know about that. Enemies? Yeah, that's about how it got to be." He looked questioningly at Jackson. "How *did* you know?"

"Doesn't matter. Go on."

"Okay. So, they got married. By that time, I was happy again. Everything was going to be fine, and I was going to have a family. Boy, I couldn't have been more wrong. Everything changed after she moved into our house. She was still sweet to me — when Dad was around. But the minute he'd go out the door she was the wicked stepmother. She'd yell at me until she got tired of that and then she'd make me go to my room and stay all day. It was worse on the days when my dad paid attention to me — any attention at all — even if he just asked me how my day had gone. That would really make her crazy-jealous. She would still be nice when he was around, but when he left the house, watch out. If I asked for anything, even a drink of water, she'd scream at me. Sometimes she slapped me, but she was always careful not to leave any marks. I got to be a nervous wreck, but I wasn't giving up on having a family. I'd still go up to her and lean against her, for affection, you know, but she'd always shove me away. It finally got to where, as soon as I'd get home from school, I'd just go on to my room." He looked at BoPeep. "Reckon I could have a drink?"

She went behind the bar and came back with a glass of ice water. He took a sip and set the glass down on the windowsill.

"The worst thing was, I'd hear her out there playing with Ashley, singing to her, watching kid shows on TV, baking cookies that I could smell but not taste."

"You're lying, boy," the sheriff said. "That ain't Marlene McBride."

"Let him finish," Jackson said.

"It was a different story when Dad got home. She would be real nice then, hugging me and smiling. I gotta tell you, I was one mixed-up little kid. See, I thought she meant it when she was nice in front of Dad. At first, I just kind of blocked out the days and lived my life in the times when

Dad was around. Those were the real times, I thought."

BoPeep shook her head. "Poor kid."

"Of course, as I got older, I couldn't fool myself any longer; I told Dad what was going on."

"And?" The sheriff leaned forward.

"And he gave me the first whipping I'd ever gotten from him. Ain't that a crock of shit?"

"It's a crock all right — if true," the sheriff said. "Go on."

"It was after that that I got really mad. I've been mad ever since. That was when I got smart. I started getting back at her. I spent all my time thinking up ways to cause her grief." He smiled bitterly. "And, boy, did I come up with some doozies. I got really good before it was over. I really laid it on the kid, too. I felt kind of bad about that sometimes. She never really did anything to me, but I hated her because Marlene loved her and despised me.

"After a while, she couldn't, or didn't want, to keep up the act any longer, so she let Dad in on the bitchy side. I guess she thought she was in so good, he'd never divorce her, or something. She'd scream and cuss at him over the least little thing. She accused him of having other women almost every day, and I saw her hit him lots of times. He'd just take it. Once, I asked him why, and he said she couldn't help herself. He was wrong. I knew she could stop; she just didn't want to. Dad must have felt guilty about me, because he started buying me stuff and spending as much time with me as he could. But it was too late. I'd already discovered what an asshole world this was, and I wasn't ever going to trust anyone again. I just played him for all I could get." He drained his glass. "I'm coming to the end now, Sheriff.

"When I was in high school, she took to disappearing for days at a time. I think it was other men, but Dad wouldn't hear that. He said she was sick. Manic-depressive. Well, maybe so, but I sure never saw her depressed. She made everybody else depressed. That was her game. When she'd done something really shitty, that's when she'd be the happiest, singing around the house, trying on makeup and new clothes. Oh, she's some piece of work. She sure is."

"That about it?" the sheriff asked.

"Just about. One more thing, though. A month before he died, Dad had had enough. He told her he wanted a divorce. That's it." He took a deep breath and folded his hands in his lap. "I hated her guts, and that's the truth. But I didn't kill my dad. Shit, he was my dad. I wouldn't hurt him." He looked from Jackson to the sheriff. "You don't believe me, do you?"

"You're mighty right I don't," the sheriff said. "How come you've been hiding out and playing games with law enforcement when you could have come in and told us this pretty little story before?"

"Because I knew she killed my dad." Three spoke slowly, as if to a child. "And I also knew he'd left everything to me in his will. Don't you think she would have gone after me in a heartbeat?"

The sheriff took the card out of his pocket. "Nice story, son. You're a regular Cinderella. But, now, I'm reading you your rights, and we're going to town."

Jackson held his hand up. "Sheriff, could I talk to you outside?"

24

Back in his office, Jackson told the sheriff about Brian Anthony's visit. He picked up the stack of papers the man had left and handed them across the desk to him.

"E-mails and letters," he said, "from Joe Junior to his brother. They go back twenty years."

He sat quietly and waited while the sheriff read the material, watching his face change as the information sank in. Finally, the sheriff looked up.

"I don't guess I need to read them all. I get the picture."

Jackson nodded. "There's a good chance Three was telling the truth."

"Looks thataway. Hell, Judge, if this feller hadn't come along, I'd've had Three in the pen before a cat could lick his ass — and slept like a baby every night."

"I know. But he did come along. And since these messages corroborate every-thing Three told us . . . listen to this." He picked up a paper from the stack. "This is from just last September. 'Brother, if it

251

wasn't for that little girl, I'd chuck it all and come to Seattle. Three's lost already. She's ruined him, made him mad at the world. And I guess I'll have to take some of the blame. I let her pull the wool over my eyes for way too long. I don't know what she'd do to her daughter if I wasn't around.' " Jackson looked up at the sheriff.

"That part, I don't understand. According to Three, she was good to her own kid."

"You didn't read everything." Jackson pawed through the stack and drew out another page. "This is from January of this year. 'Today, she turned on Ashley again — slapped her across the face with a hairbrush. Told her she was fat and ugly. The poor kid left for school with a ton of makeup on to cover up the mark her own mother had left on her cheek. Brother, I just don't know how that girl stays so sweet and pleasant in the face of all she's going through. I'd take her away with me, but what court would give a girl child to a stepfather? Marlene would fight it, of course, and she's one hell of a good actress. There's not a soul outside of these walls that knows what hell we go through. The whole town thinks she's just perfect. No, brother, I'm trapped here.' "

"My God!" the sheriff said.

"What?"

"This means she's probably done away with Ashley, her own daughter. I'm stumped. You got any ideas on what our next move should be?"

"I'm not so sure she's done away with Ashley. If she has, where's the body?" He leaned back in his chair. "Think about it. In the other two murders, there was no attempt to hide the bodies. They were left where they died."

"Good point," the sheriff said.

"There's also the fact that she's a small woman, and Ashley's a large girl. I don't believe Marlene could move her body."

"Suppose she took her off somewhere and killed her."

"There's always that possibility, but Mae's been keeping a close watch on Marlene."

"So, what do I do?"

"Well, you could pick her up and charge her now." He paused. "But, if she's keeping Ashley alive somewhere, we'd be smarter to watch her. I don't think she'd tell us a thing if we brought her in. And the child may be locked up somewhere." He paused. "There's no hurry. I've got a feeling she thinks she's winning this game and has no intention of running away."

Just then, the intercom buzzed. Jackson punched the button. "What?"

"You don't have to bite my head off." Edna was aggrieved. "Patty called. She's gone home with Kristi."

"Who's Kristi?"

"She said you'd know — the new kid that's moved in over at the Largents'."

"Okay. That all?"

"She wants you to pick her up on your way home."

"Got it." Jackson clicked off the machine and turned back to the sheriff. "Have you got anybody besides Dooley you can put on this?"

The sheriff nodded. "The DA's hired an investigator. Waste of money, if you ask me, but you know Shelby Grayson. He's got big-city ideas." He shifted in his chair. "Feller sits around the office most of the time, not doing anything but drawing his paycheck. I'll see if they'll let me borrow him."

"ASAP," Jackson said.

The sheriff gave a thumbs-up sign and left the room.

Jackson lit a Don Diego and then started in on the paperwork that had accumulated on his desk. He worked steadily for two hours and was surprised when Edna pushed open the door carrying her purse.

"It's six, Jackson. I'm going home. Don't forget your daughter."

"Thanks. Guess I'd better go, too." He closed the file he was working on.

Edna remained in the doorway.

"What?"

"What's going on, Jackson?"

"Can't say right now. You'll know in the next day or so."

"Well, shit." She turned and left the office.

Jackson smiled after her. He had tried every way he knew to clean up her language, but so far he hadn't made much headway.

It was almost six when Jackson pulled his car into the driveway at the Rice mansion. He drove around to the back of the huge brownstone house and parked under the carport. He waved to three little girls who were playing with Barbie dolls on the back porch. They smiled back shyly. He opened the door and went into the kitchen. Nobody ever bothered to knock there since the place had become a foster home. Most people just walked into the kitchen and yelled, hoping to be heard over the din the children made.

Vanessa and Myrtice Rice were sitting at

the kitchen table drinking iced tea. In the background he heard the television blaring, and in another room someone was practicing the piano. A pot roast cooking in the oven filled the room with delicious smells.

"Jackson." Vanessa smiled up at him. "Sit down and have a glass of tea with us. Patty's not ready to go home yet. Tell us all the latest news."

"Thanks." Jackson accepted the frosty glass Myrtice handed him. "Can't stay long. Lutie'll be mad if we're late for supper." He took a seat at the table. "Hear anything from Ray?"

Myrtice sighed. "It's just so sad," she said. "He doesn't understand why he has to be in that place." Her voice cracked. "And I miss him so much."

Jackson shook his head, not knowing what to say.

Vanessa covered the older woman's hand with her own. "We can go there and bring him back," she said. "We'll hire somebody to watch him if we have to." She looked at Jackson. "She's having a real hard time with this."

"It could be done," Jackson said. "Medicare might even help pay for it."

Myrtice got up and took a paper towel

from the roll under the cabinets. She wiped her eyes and blew her nose. "I don't know, Jackson. I just couldn't take any more of that running away all the time."

"Did you ever figure out where he was going?"

"We did, actually. And it was not far, thank the good Lord. Just across the street to that vacant lot next to Marlene's house."

"Why do you think he went over there?"

Vanessa went to the counter and took some oatmeal cookies from a cookie jar shaped like a fat baker. She put them on a plate and set them on the table. "One won't spoil your supper," she said, sliding the plate toward Jackson.

Jackson took a cookie. "Did you know why he was going over there?" he repeated.

"Oh, Jackson, Alzheimer's is a horrible disease," Vanessa said. "He probably didn't even know himself."

"He knew, or at least he thought he did." Myrtice spoke up. "He said he had to go look after the baby."

"The baby?"

"Well, you know, in his mind, I guess there was a baby over there."

"It could have been a baby bird — or kittens," Vanessa suggested.

"Well, as if that wasn't enough, then there was all that stealing!" She nodded vigorously, her gray curls bouncing up and down.

"Myrtice, now we've talked about that — it wasn't really stealing," Vanessa said. "Oh, here comes Steve. Hi, honey." She stood up as her husband entered the room.

"Got that toilet fixed," he said, giving Vanessa a quick hug. "Hi, Jackson. Didn't know you were here." He pulled up a chair and joined them at the table. "Any chance of getting a glass of that tea?"

Myrtice poured tea over ice and handed the glass to him before sitting back down. "We were just telling Jackson about how Ray used to steal."

"You told me about that at the courthouse," Jackson reminded her.

"A few candy bars," Steve said. "We can afford it." He laughed. "No big deal."

"It's the principle," Myrtice said. "He wasn't raised that way. And he wouldn't even admit he was eating them. Said they were for the baby. Imagine! Then, the minute my back was turned, off he'd go to that vacant lot."

"Why? I wonder," Jackson mused.

"Don't ask me. Second childhood, I guess. There's nothing over there except that old fall-out shelter that Fred Dickson built back in '59."

"I remember my dad talking about that," Jackson said. "He called it Dickson's Folly."

"Everybody called it that," Myrtice said. "Fred Dickson was a very odd person. He was just sure the Russians were planning to drop an A-bomb right on top of little Post Oak, Texas."

"What happened to him?" Jackson wanted to know.

Myrtice picked up a cookie and took a bite. "The house burned down in 1970. Burned to the ground, not a thing left but the foundation. They moved away right after that, just abandoned the place. The city finally had to come in and clean up the mess. Now, all that's left is the shelter."

"We tried to buy it once," Steve said. "Problem is, you can't get a clear title because nobody knows where the Dicksons moved to. Eventually, the city will take it for the taxes, I guess."

"Here's something odd about the place," Vanessa said. "Some nights, I can't sleep, so I go out and sit on the balcony off our bedroom. I like to watch the stars."

"It faces that lot," Steve put in.

"And I would see a ghostly figure

moving across that lot." Vanessa laughed. "Steve said I was crazy, and he was right."

"Why?"

"Well, one night, I was sitting out there, there was a full moon and, sure enough, here came the ghostly figure — only it wasn't a ghost at all. It was Marlene, wearing her nightgown. She went straight to that fall-out shelter and went inside. Don't you think she needs to be seen by a psychiatrist, Jackson?"

But Jackson didn't hear. He already had his cell phone out and was dialing the sheriff's number.

25

Ashley lay curled up in a ball on her cot. She was so very hungry. Hard as she tried, she couldn't remember when she had eaten last. Was it two days ago — or maybe, three? She knew she had watched the sun rise at least twice, maybe more. Her mind wasn't as clear as it used to be.

In the dampness, she had developed a cough. Her throat was dry and sore. She felt cold some of the time, and huddled under the thin blanket. Other times, she burned with fever, and sweat would pour from her body when it broke. What if I die here? She wondered. Will they ever find my body? Will I be a skeleton? She shuddered. Dying was on her mind a lot lately, dying and food. She rolled over and lowered her feet to the floor. She stood up, but when she did, nausea swept over her; her head swam. She sat back down and waited until the dizziness went away. She made her way slowly to the sink. She turned on the water, put her head under the faucet and drank for a long time. The water didn't stay down, and she vomited it back into the sink. Back on her cot, she lay still, staring into the darkness. She felt better after the vomiting.

She wondered what Patty was doing now. Since she had no idea of the time, it would be impossible to guess, so she pretended it was suppertime, and Patty was sitting at the kitchen table with Lutie and her dad. Maybe Judge Crain had just told one of his lame jokes, and they were all laughing — or maybe Patty was filling them in on all the latest gossip from Post Oak Middle School.

She pictured the food on the table. She conjured up Lutie Faye's famous chicken and dumplings, warm and creamy, with white dumplings, light as air, floating above tender chunks of white chicken. She could almost smell it. And on the counter, she saw a peach pie, buttery-sweet and a little tart, with sugar and cinnamon sprinkled on the top crust.

She guessed the foam party must have already come and gone. She hated having missed it. It seemed ages ago, the day they had talked about whether Patty should go with Sonny Smart or whether she should go with the girls. Ashley hoped she had gone with Sonny. He was so gone over her. She was getting sleepy again. Maybe an angel would come and take her to heaven while she slept.

She slept hard, and when she opened her eyes, she saw a beautiful, bright light shining down on her. She wasn't surprised, only peaceful. The angel had come for her. She lay very still, closed her eyes, and waited to float out of her body and into the light.

Nothing happened.

And then in that instant, chaos erupted. A door banged. She heard running feet, shouts, and the sound of a scuffle.

Ashley fainted.

26

When Ashley opened her eyes again, she found herself tucked into a clean, white bed. It felt like heaven, but when she looked around her, she knew that it wasn't heaven; it was a hospital room. She saw a plastic bag suspended above her, dripping liquid into a tube. She followed the tube with her eyes and saw that it was attached to her wrist with a bit of white tape. Looking down at her hand, she saw something that surprised her. A large and very warm hand was holding hers. The hand was comforting. She dozed off. When she woke again, the hand was still there. Sleepily, she glanced up to see whose hand it was. She froze.

The hand belonged to Three. She tried to jerk free, but he held on tight.

"Easy, little sister," he said. "I'm not going to hurt you."

"That's for sure," announced a large black nurse who had just come into the room. "This boy hasn't left your side for two whole days."

Ashley looked up at Three. "Really?"

"Really."

"Why?" was all she could think of to say.

"Well, the way I've got it figured, I'm all you've got, and you're all I've got, now. Your mom's dead, honey."

"How?"

"They told me she took a whole bottle of pills just before she tried to kill you."

Ashley winced.

"You sure you want to hear this, now?"

"Yes. Tell me."

"Okay. See, she tried to kill both of you with the pills — a murder-suicide. She put the pills in your milk, a lot of them, but they didn't seem to phase you."

"I didn't drink the milk."

"I see. Well, that explains that."

"How do you know all that — about the pills, I mean?"

"She talked to the sheriff and Judge Crain before the medicine kicked in. About thirty minutes went by before her voice started to slur and the judge realized what she must have done. They rushed her to the hospital, but it was too late. She'd taken a lot of pills, hon."

A tear rolled down Ashley's face.

He squeezed her hand. "She was sick, little sister."

Ashley searched his face. "I wonder what will happen to me."

"I've been thinking about that, too, and I've come up with a plan. Want to hear it?"

Ashley nodded.

"Okay. Dad left everything to me. Did you know that?"

"No."

"Well, I was thinking that me and you could just go on living in the house. I could get a job and you could finish school. We'd be, like . . . well . . . our own little family of two."

"You'd do that?"

He nodded.

Ashley closed her eyes.

"You get some rest now," Three said. "I'll go down the hall and try to talk the nurses into giving me a cup of coffee."

Ashley nodded.

He extricated his hand from hers and stood up. As he was opening the door, she spoke again.

"Three?"

"Yes."

"You had it wrong when you said Mama was sick. She wasn't sick; she was mean and selfish. She never loved anyone but herself."

"I call that sick," he said. "Now, you get some rest."

27

On Memorial Day, Vanessa Largent decided to hold a backyard barbecue. It was time, she said, to get past the gloomy mood a lot of folks had gotten themselves into over the McBride family deaths. It would be a big party. The inhabitants of the Rice mansion alone made eleven. There were Vanessa and her husband, Steve, their seven foster children, and Myrtice and Ray Rice.

Myrtice had grieved so much that Steve finally called the hospital and asked their advice on bringing Ray back. The doctors said he would certainly do better at home, as long as the family found someone to be with him at all times. Steve had a brilliant idea.

"We'll ask Three to do it," he said.

"Yes!" Vanessa thought that was a wonderful idea. "Three needs something to do that's productive," she said. "This will be the very thing."

Three had agreed to take the job — on a temporary basis only, as he planned on enrolling in the local community college in September.

They invited everyone they could think of who might be depressed by recent events, and then they invited others because, as Steve said, it's just as easy to cook for a large crowd as for a small one. Jackson Crain came with Patty; Sheriff Gibbs was there with his wife, Norma Jean; Mae Applewaite came with the two Archer cousins and Annabeth Jones. At the last minute, Vanessa decided to ask Horace Kinkaid and his wife, Pauline, because, as Steve said, it would just about kill him if he were left out. Edna Buchannan came but left her husband at home. Rip Clark showed up uninvited, bringing Brian Anthony with him. Mandy d'Alejandro was not invited. Vanessa hated to leave her out, but she wasn't sure just what was going on between Mandy and Jackson, and she didn't want to be the cause of an awkward situation.

Steve strung red, white, and blue lights in the trees in the yard. He set up long folding tables for the adults under the porte cochere. The older girls decorated them with red plastic tablecloths and potted ivy with little American flags tucked in among the leaves. Separate tables for the smaller children stood nearby. Steve cooked chicken, sausage, and big slabs of pork ribs in the pit outside, while the women made all the trimmings in the kitchen.

The adults sat under the trees in lawn chairs sipping drinks and enjoying the smell of the roasting meat. The conversation turned to the thing that was still on everyone's minds.

Mae opened the subject. "Jackson, I just don't understand why it all happened. Marlene was such a quiet little thing."

"And so pretty," Pauline Kinkaid said.

"Still water runs deep," Annabeth put in.

"Dark water's a better word." Horace sipped his beer. "There was something . . ."

"Ugly," Jane Archer said. "There's no other word for it."

Everybody nodded.

"But why? That's what I can't get my head around," Mae persisted.

"Brian can answer that," Jackson said.

"My brother was going to leave her. Anybody mind if I smoke?" He didn't wait for an answer, simply took a pipe out of his shirt pocket and proceeded to fill and light it.

"I love the smell of a pipe," Esther said. "My daddy smoked one. Remember, Jane?"

Jane nodded but spoke to Brian. "You

mean he was going to divorce her?"

"No, just leave. He was going to take Ashley with him."

"That's crazy," Horace said. "She wasn't even his daughter."

"Crazy, maybe, but he was desperate. My brother was a tenderhearted guy, too tenderhearted. I'm just telling you the story the way he told it to me. For the past two years, Marlene's violent behavior had escalated to the point where he feared for his life; Ashley's, too. He knew he had to get out, but he couldn't bring himself to leave the girl behind." He shook his head. "He said the abuse started out verbal, but soon escalated into slapping and pushing. He could see the child's confidence fading away under the weight of it. His words, not mine." He put back his head and blew a line of smoke rings into the air.

"So, he just decided to take the kid and go? That doesn't make a damn bit of sense." Not waiting for an answer, Rip got up and joined Steve at the barbecue pit.

Brian answered his question anyway. "Only after something else happened. Jackson can tell you about that."

Jackson nodded. "She had decided to divorce him. He must have found out about it; maybe she told him. Anyway, if he let that happen, she would have Ashley all to herself."

"A man can't just run off with somebody's kid," Sheriff Gibbs said. "He'd be found and thrown in jail, for sure."

"Then where would the poor young'un be?" demanded Edna. "Right back with her mama. What the hell was he thinking?"

"He was well aware of that," Brian continued. "He had a plan, you see. He was going to take her to Australia."

"Australia! Get out," Horace shot back.

"It's not as strange as it sounds. You see, we still have family there. They run a sheep station in the outback."

"A sheep station?" Jane asked.

"It's like a ranch. Anyway, he'd been communicating with our cousins for a long time. I was the one who put him in touch with them. I've visited them several times. They're good people. They urged Joe to come to them, said they could hide him and Ashley."

"They'd still be found," the sheriff insisted.

"Not necessarily." Brian got up and took another beer from the cooler. "There's more. You see, we've got this one cousin. Oh, he's straight now, but he used to operate outside the law. He did jail time in Sidney for racketeering. Seven years, actually — and when he came out, he made up his mind to straighten his life out. He joined his brother in the sheep business. Thing was, he still had a few contacts. He could arrange to get Joe and the girl fake identification, no problem."

"Sounds like a pretty crazy scheme to me," Horace said.

"My brother was a desperate man, and as I said before, too tenderhearted. He had seen his son ruined; he refused to let that happen to the little girl."

"So, was he just going to go off and leave Three here? I can't believe that, after he spoiled him so." This was Norma Jean Gibbs.

"He had an idea that his leaving might bring Three around."

"How was that supposed to happen?" Mae wanted to know.

"It was a sink-or-swim kind of thing. Like, if Joe wasn't around to clean up his messes, Three might just learn to stand on his own feet. Am I right?" asked Annabeth.

"Something like that. Joe knew something had to change — and he just never could bring himself to cut the boy off. Whatever his reasoning was, he already had the tickets and was planning to get out in a matter of days."

"And then he was murdered," Jane said. "She must have known."

"I think she did. Apparently, she went into his computer and read his e-mail. I warned him to get a secure password, but he insisted that she wasn't interested in that sort of thing." Brian knocked out his pipe on a rock. "And that's the end of that story. She killed him while he slept."

Suddenly, Edna pointed to a group standing under some trees. "Good God A'mighty! Speak of the devil!"

A tall, beautiful redhead stood talking to Patty, Sonny Smart and Kristi. She threw back her head and laughed at something Sonny had said. There was no mistaking that laugh.

"My soul, it can't be her!" Esther put her hand to her heart.

"That's not Marlene," Jackson said. "It's Ashley."

"No, it's not." Jane was adamant. "Ashley's a chubby girl."

"Remember, she almost starved while Marlene had her locked up," Jackson reminded them.

"Will wonders never cease?" Mae said. "I never thought she looked a bit like her mama." Suddenly she pointed to the house. "Well, looky here, it's Ray and Three."

Three was holding the back door open for Ray to make his slow way out. He took the old man's arm and propelled him to a lawn chair next to the barbecue so he could watch Steve cook.

"I hear that boy's going to college this fall," Annabeth said. "He may turn out well after all."

"Barber college is where he ought to go," Horace put in. "All the McBrides have been barbers. It's in their blood."

The sheriff's hand went to a bare spot in his left sideburn. "Speaking of blood, that little lady barber just about cut my face off when she gave me a trim last week."

"She can't cut hair worth a dime," Horace agreed.

Pauline nodded. "She's got Horace looking like Friar Tuck." She grinned.

"She's left town," Jackson said.

"Do tell," Mae murmured.

"How come you get to know everything, Jackson?" Horace griped. "I'm supposed to be the newspaperman around here."

Just then Rip walked up. "If you'd stay out of my place and get out on the street once in a while, you might find out something. Where's she going, Judge?"

"To California," Jackson said. "I stopped by the shop the other day and she was packing her things. She's got a job offer out there. She left this morning."

"End of an era," Annabeth said. "I can't remember when there hasn't been a barbershop in that spot. I guess you men will all have to join us ladies at the Cut 'n' Curl."

Just then, Vanessa walked up with a tray of bacon-wrapped shrimp. "Dinner's not for another hour," she apologized. "Steve forgot to thaw the meat." She laughed. "Have something to tide you over."

"We were just admiring Ashley," Pauline said. "She's just beautiful."

"Isn't she? But she's always been that way inside." Vanessa smiled. "We're so happy she's going to live here with us."

"Last I heard, Three was wanting to keep her home with him," Horace said. "Change his mind?"

"Yes, he did." Vanessa set down the tray and pulled up a folding chair. "We all sat down and discussed it last night and all agreed that she would be happier here. I think Three was a little relieved. After all, he had community college coming up in the fall, and maybe university later." She reached for the glass of wine Jackson had poured for her. "It's amazing how that boy has changed." She sipped her wine. "Or maybe he hasn't changed so much. Maybe it's just that we didn't know him very well."

The others nodded.

Jackson saw Patty coming toward him, followed by Kristi and Ashley. "Daddy, can I spend the night here? Please, say yes. Kristi says there's an extra bed in her room."

Jackson raised his eyebrows. "An extra bed? In this house?" He looked at Vanessa.

"Well, a trundle bed," she laughed. "But she's welcome to stay."

"Then it's fine with me," Jackson said.

After the girls had left, their arms around each other's waists, Horace had more questions.

"Okay. So, we know why she killed Joe. But, what I'm still asking myself is, why did she have to go and kill old Gerald?"

Jackson spoke. "That was a spur-of-the moment act. Three had come to the foam party. He talked to Gerald outside the boat-house. Patty saw it, and I'm sure she wasn't the only one. Marlene probably heard the kids talking about it and got suspicious. She would want to know what those two had to talk about." He lit a Don Diego and blew a puff of smoke sideways, away from the women. "We know now that Three told him that he believed Marlene had killed Joe."

"Gerald wouldn't have believed it," Mae said. "He's been in love with Marlene since high school. Course, she never gave him a second glance. Everybody knew that."

The others nodded.

"She must have decided not to take any chances."

"What a shame," Esther put in. "Gerald would never have believed she was a murderer."

"That's right," Annabeth said. "The man was plumb blind when it came to her."

"How do you know all that?" Norma Jean was curious. She was too busy at the jail to get in on the town gossip.

"Honey, everybody knew how Gerald felt about his sister-in-law," Mae said. "You ought to get out more."

"By the way, Mae," Jackson said. "Did you call Marlene and ask her to find your wallet?"

"My wallet?" Mae was indignant. "I don't even own a wallet. I keep my money in a coin purse, just like my mother did."

"Oh, I see Steve's taking the meat off the grill," Vanessa said. "I reckon we're going to eat sooner than I thought."

It was well after ten when the party

ended. Jackson was tired. He decided to go to bed right away, so he could get an early start on that paperwork Edna had been nagging him about.

As he pulled his car into the carport behind his house, he noticed that a light had been left on in his den. Lutie Faye must have forgotten to turn it off when she left. He opened the screen door and stepped onto the back porch. He stopped suddenly when he heard the chains on the porch swing creak.

"Who's there?"

"I didn't figure on you being this late." Lutie's voice came from the darkness.

"What are you doing here?"

"I thought I'd just make jam out of that crate of berries you brought home. They were going to spoil."

"So, are you finished?"

"Um-hmm."

"Then what are you doing here? Why don't you go home?"

"I am, now."

Jackson waited.

"I didn't like to leave while you had a guest in the house."

Jackson's shoulders slumped. "Who is it?"

"Go on and see." She got up and headed

for the door. "I'll see you in the morning."

Jackson took a deep breath. He was furious with Lutie for letting someone wait for him until this hour. She should have told them to see him in his office in the morning. This wasn't the first time strangers had come to his home. Sometimes, they wanted to get married; other times they came to convince him to get a relative out of jail or give a favorable ruling in some case or other. He was glad to perform the marriage ceremonies, provided the paperwork was in order. But the others he sent packing. Tonight, he hoped it was the latter. He was too tired even to read the marriage ceremony.

He strode down the hall, determined to get rid of the intruder in no time flat. He opened the den door and stepped inside. The light from the floor lamp spilled down on his old leather club chair and on the figure that was curled up in it.

"What took you so long?" Mandy said. She held out her arms to him.

ABOUT THE AUTHOR

NANCY BELL is a fifth-generation Texan. She spends her time between Austin and her hometown of Pittsburg, Texas, where she draws inspiration for her novels. She is currently working on the third Jackson Crain novel.